"What am I d..." demanded.

"Why did the King of Bahania ask me to come here? And what are *you* doing here?"

Reyhan stared at her. His strong, handsome features were unreadable.

"Haven't you guessed?" he asked with quiet amusement. "The king is my father, and the invitation was as much mine as his. I am Prince Reyhan...."

He kept on talking, but she didn't hear him. "A p-prince?" she asked, stumbling over the word. He couldn't be. A prince? Him? But they'd met at college. They'd dated. They'd—

"The king decided it was time for me to marry," Reyhan told her. "But there was no way I could agree to any match as I was already married. To you."

Dear Reader,

Well, it's that time of year again—and if those beautiful buds of April are any indication, you're in the mood for love! And what better way to sustain that mood than with our latest six Special Edition novels? We open the month with the latest installment of Sherryl Woods's MILLION DOLLAR DESTINIES series, *Priceless.* When a pediatric oncologist who deals with life and death on a daily basis meets a sick child's football hero, she thinks said hero can make the little boy's dreams come true. But little does she know that he can make hers a reality, as well! Don't miss this compelling story....

MERLYN COUNTY MIDWIVES continues with Maureen Child's *Forever...Again,* in which a man who doesn't believe in second chances has a change of mind—not to mention heart—when he meets the beautiful new public relations guru at the midwifery clinic. In *Cattleman's Heart* by Lois Faye Dyer, a businesswoman assigned to help a struggling rancher finds that business is the last thing on her mind when she sees the shirtless cowboy meandering toward her! And Susan Mallery's popular DESERT ROGUES are back! In *The Sheik & the Princess in Waiting,* a woman learns that the man she loved in college has two secrets: 1) he's a prince; and 2) they're married! Next, can a pregnant earthy vegetarian chef find happiness with town's resident playboy, an admitted carnivore... and father of her child? Find out in *The Best of Both Worlds* by Elissa Ambrose. And in Vivienne Wallington's *In Her Husband's Image,* a widow confronted with her late husband's twin brother is forced to decide, as she looks in the eyes of her little boy, if some secrets are worth keeping.

So enjoy the beginnings of spring, and all six of these wonderful books! And don't forget to come back next month for six new compelling reads from Silhouette Special Edition.

Happy reading!

Gail Chasan
Senior Editor

Please address questions and book requests to:
Silhouette Reader Service
U.S.: 3010 Walden Ave., P.O. Box 1325, Buffalo, NY 14269
Canadian: P.O. Box 609, Fort Erie, Ont. L2A 5X3

Susan Mallery

THE SHEIK & THE PRINCESS IN WAITING

Silhouette®

SPECIAL EDITION®

Published by Silhouette Books

America's Publisher of Contemporary Romance

SILHOUETTE BOOKS

ISBN 0-373-24606-4

THE SHEIK & THE PRINCESS IN WAITING

Copyright © 2004 by Susan Macias Redmond

This edition published by arrangement with Harlequin Books S.A.

® and TM are trademarks of Harlequin Books S.A., used under license. Trademarks indicated with ® are registered in the United States Patent and Trademark Office, the Canadian Trade Marks Office and in other countries.

Visit Silhouette at www.eHarlequin.com

Printed in U.S.A.

Books by Susan Mallery

SUSAN MALLERY

is the bestselling and award-winning author of over fifty books for Harlequin and Silhouette Books. She makes her home in California with her handsome prince of a husband and her two adorable-but-not-bright cats.

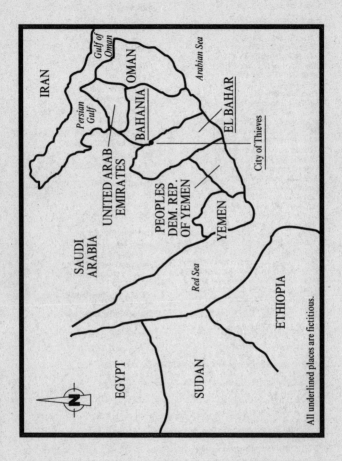

All underlined places are fictitious.

Chapter One

After a long day of working in the delivery room, Emma Kennedy was ready to spend her evening with her feet propped up, the TV on and a bowl of ice cream in her hand. Okay, yes, she would probably eat something decent for dinner first but the ice cream was a must. It had been *that* kind of day.

Nothing had happened all morning, then right at noon, four women had decided to deliver. One had been a terrified teenager, and Emma had stayed with her as much as possible. At twenty-four, Emma had been closest in age of all the nurses, although a lifetime of experiences away from the street-wise, body pierced and tattooed patient.

Emma opened her mailbox, pulled out the cable bill

and a flyer for a sale at Dillard's, then walked toward her apartment.

She was tired, but content. It had been a good day. A happy day. One of the things she loved about her job was the joy new mothers experienced when their babies were born. Being part of the process, even on the periphery, was all the thanks she needed. When she thought about all the—

Emma suddenly stopped in the hallway. Two men in dark suits stood by her front door. They looked respectable enough—clean, short haircuts, polished shoes—but they were definitely *lurking*.

She'd taken several self-defense courses over the years, but she wasn't sure how helpful the information she'd learned would be against two large men.

Glancing first left, then right, she calculated the distance to her nearest neighbor. How long would it take her to run to her car, and what kind of reaction she would get if she screamed?

One of the men looked up and saw her. "Ms. Kennedy? I'm Alex Dunnard from the State Department. This is my associate, Jack Sanders. May we have a moment of your time?"

As the man spoke, he pulled out an ID card complete with picture. His companion did the same. Emma abandoned the idea of bolting and approached her front door.

The pictures matched the men and the cards *looked* official enough, but it wasn't as if she'd seen a State Department ID before and would know the difference.

Alex Dunnard slipped the ID back into his jacket pocket and smiled. "We have some official business to discuss with you. May we come inside, or would you be more comfortable if we met at the coffee shop on the corner?''

Emma noticed that neither option allowed her to get out of talking with them. Which was crazy. What would the State Department want with her?

She gave them the once-over and decided to let them in. Her Dallas suburb was safe, quiet and ordinary. No doubt these men had the wrong person. Once they straightened that out, they would be on their way.

''Come on in,'' she said, inserting her key in the lock.

They followed her into the smallish living room. It was already dusk, so she turned on both floor lamps and the light in the hall, then motioned to her sofa.

''Have a seat,'' she said as she plopped down in the club chair opposite.

As she set her purse on the floor, she noticed several stains on the front of her brightly patterned scrub shirt. The pale green pants were also dotted and streaked. Occupational hazard, she reminded herself.

Alex perched on the edge of her sofa, while the other gentleman stood by the sliding glass door.

''Ms. Kennedy, we're here at the behest of the king of Bahania.''

Alex kept on talking, but Emma was too caught up in the word *behest.* She wasn't sure she'd ever heard someone say it in normal speech. It was more of a book word. Then the rest of the sentence sunk in.

''Wait a minute,'' she said, holding up her hand. ''Did you say the *king* of Bahania?''

"Yes, ma'am. He contacted the State Department and asked that we locate you and then offer you an official invitation to visit his country."

Emma laughed. Oh, sure. Because that sort of thing happened all the time. "Are you guys selling something? Because if you are, you're wasting your time."

"No, ma'am. We're from the State Department, and we're here—"

She cut him off with a wave. "I know. At the behest. I got that part. You have the wrong person. I'm sure there's another Emma Kennedy floating around who has lots of personal contact with His Royal Highness, but it's not me."

She looked at her modest apartment. If only, she thought humorously. Maybe a small money grant or two could have taken care of her student loans. And she desperately needed new tires for her ten-year-old import. Oh, well. In her next life she would be rich. In this one she was just a single woman struggling to pay the bills.

Alex pulled a piece of paper out of his outer jacket pocket. "Emma Kennedy," he read, then went on to list her birth date, place of birth, her parents' names and the number on her passport. A passport she'd had since she was eighteen, young, innocent and foolish and had thought... Well, she'd thought a lot of things.

"Just a second," she said, and rose to walk into her bedroom.

Her passport was tucked in the back of her sock drawer. She pulled it out and returned to the living room where she had Alex read the number again. It matched.

"This is creepy," she said. "Look, I don't know the king of Bahania. I'm not sure I could find Bahania on the map. There really has to be some kind of mistake. What would he want with me?"

"You are to be his guest for the next two weeks." Alex stood and smiled. "There's a private jet standing by to take you to his country. Ms. Kennedy, Bahania is a valuable ally in the Middle East. Like their neighbor, El Bahar, they are considered the Switzerland of that region. These progressive countries offer a haven of peace and economic stability in a troubled part of the world. They also provide a significant percentage of our country's oil."

Emma might have only taken one political science class at college, but she wasn't stupid. She got the message. When the king of Bahania invited a young Texas nurse to vacation in his country for a couple of weeks, the United States government expected her to go.

Was she being kidnapped?

The idea was both insane and terrifying.

"You can't make me go," she said, more to hear the words than because she believed them. She had a feeling that Alex and his friend could make her do just about anything.

"You're correct. We would not force you to accept the king's invitation. However, your country would be most grateful if you would consider granting him this request." He smiled. "You'll be perfectly safe, Ms. Kennedy. The king is an honorable man. You're not being sold into a harem."

"The thought never crossed my mind," she told him hotly, even though it had. Sort of.

A harem? Her? Not on this planet. Men didn't find her especially appealing, and she... Well, she avoided matters of the heart. She'd fallen in love once and it had been a complete disaster.

"This is a great honor," Alex said. "As a personal guest of the king, you'll be staying at the famed pink palace. It is quite extraordinary."

Emma walked back to her chair and sank down. "Can we stop for a second and reflect on the reality missing from this situation? I'm a nurse. I deliver babies for a living. Unless the king has a pregnant wife or something, why on earth would he be interested in me? I'm assuming if you know my passport number, you also know I've only been out of the country once and that was six years ago. I live a quiet life. I'm boring. You have the wrong person."

Alex's good cheer didn't waiver. "Two weeks, Ms. Kennedy. Is that so much to ask? Those volunteering for military service give much more."

Oh, darn the man. He was going for guilt. She really didn't like that. Her parents had been experts at it and she hated the sense of having disappointed anyone.

"I'll accompany you to Bahania," Alex continued. "To assure your safe arrival. Once you're settled, I'll return to Washington." He paused. "You're being given a wonderful opportunity, Ms. Kennedy. I hope you'll consider it. If we can leave for the airport in the next hour, we will be in Bahania by sunset tomorrow."

Her mind swirled. ''You want me to go with you right now?''

''Please.''

Emma glanced from Alex to his friend by the sliding glass door. She had a bad feeling that if she refused, she would be taken against her will. Not exactly thoughts to warm her heart. It looked as if she were going on a trip.

Two and a half hours later, Emma found herself sitting on a luxurious private jet as the lights of Dallas disappeared below. She had a large suitcase in the cargo bay, a small overnight case next to her feet and, as promised, Alex Dunnard in the seat across from hers.

She still wasn't sure how it had all happened. Somehow Alex had gently ushered her through the process of calling the hospital for time off, packing and leaving a message for her parents that she'd gone away with a friend. The white lie had been his suggestion, made so that her parents wouldn't worry.

Then she'd showered, changed and found herself in a limo the size of a football field. Now she was on a plane and sitting in leather seats so soft and comfy, she wouldn't mind having the material made into a jacket.

On the bright side, if she *was* being kidnapped, it was by someone with money and style. The downside was that she'd managed to put her entire life on hold for two weeks with exactly two phone calls and a request that her neighbor pick up her mail. What did that say about her world?

Before she could decide, a uniformed young woman approached. "Ms. Kennedy, I'm Aneesa and it will be my pleasure to serve you on our flight to Bahania."

Aneesa rattled off the expected flying time, mentioned a stop for gas in Spain and offered selections for dinner.

"When you're ready to retire for the evening," she continued, "there is a sleeping compartment for your use." She smiled. "Along with a bathroom, complete with shower."

"That's great," Emma told her, trying to sound calm. As if this sort of thing happened to her all the time.

"Shall I serve dinner?" Aneesa asked.

"Uh, sure. Why not?"

When the attendant had disappeared to what must be the plane's galley, Emma turned to Alex.

"Are you going to tell me what's really going on here?" she asked.

"I've told you all I know."

"That the king wants me as his guest for two weeks," she summarized.

"Yes."

"And you don't know why?"

"No."

Not exactly helpful.

She returned her attention to the countryside below and wondered if she would ever see Texas again. Then, determined not to wallow in unpleasant and scary thoughts, she pulled out the entertainment guide and pretended interest in the various DVDs available for her viewing pleasure.

A half hour later, the meal was served. The food was beautifully prepared and delicious, if Alex's speed of consumption was anything to go by. Emma picked at the baked chicken dish and refused wine. She studied her travel companion—a well-dressed man in his mid to late forties. Nice looking, married— if the wedding ring was anything to go by. Did Mrs. Dunnard mind her husband flying off at a moment's notice? Had it been a moment's notice for him or had he known about the trip in advance? And why on earth did the king of Bahania want to meet with *her?*

More questions she was unlikely to get answered. When she tried pumping Alex for information, he remained pleasant but uncommunicative.

One restless night in a luxury cabin, several time zones and a pit stop for gas later, Emma didn't know any more than she had when she'd stepped onto the plane in Dallas. The difference was they were coming in for landing at an airport on the edge of the desert.

She stared out the window and tried to keep her mouth from falling open. The sights beneath were so beautiful they nearly took her breath away.

Turquoise-blue water lapped up against a pure white beach. There were miles of buildings, lush foliage and sprawling suburbs that gradually gave way to the endless beige and browns of the desert. Emma could see pockets of industry, large buildings that appeared ancient and what looked like dozens of parks throughout the city before the plane banked and headed for the airport.

They landed with a light bump, then taxied to a low one-story building. As Alex picked up his small overnight case, Emma fumbled for her purse.

She was escorted onto the tarmac where the late afternoon was warm, sunny and dry. And bright. After the confines of the plane, she found the sunlight nearly blinding. Three steps later, she entered a pleasant room where a man in uniform actually bowed when she presented herself and her open passport.

"Ms. Kennedy," he said, flashing a smile, "welcome to Bahania. May your journey be pleasant and blessed."

"Thank you," she murmured, wondering if everyone was always so polite. Not that she was going to complain. She could get used to this level of service.

The surprises weren't over. Minutes later Alex escorted her to another large limo. Inside she found a bottle of champagne sitting on ice and a small bouquet of flowers.

"For me?" she asked as Alex sat next to her.

"I doubt the king meant them for me," he told her.

Good point. Emma sniffed the roses. When Alex pointed to the bottle of champagne, she shook her head.

"I didn't sleep," she admitted. "Between being exhausted, the strange circumstances and the time change, the last thing I need is liquor."

She already felt woozy enough.

As they pulled out of the airport, Alex began to talk to her about the city. He pointed out the financial district, the old shopping bazaar, the entrance to the famous Bahanian beaches. Emma did her best to pay attention, but the longer they were on the road, the more she regretted her decision to come. Sure, Bahania was beautiful and all, but she'd just traveled halfway around the world with a man she didn't know to meet a king she'd barely heard of, and aside from her traveling companion and the king, no one on the planet knew where she was.

It was not a situation designed to make one relax.

Forty minutes later, the limo drove through an open gate, past several guards and what felt like miles of manicured grounds. She stared out the window until she saw the first hints of the fabled pink palace.

"This is so not happening," she murmured, still unable to believe this was real.

The limo pulled up in front of the entrance. At least she assumed that's what the arched doorway and alcove big enough for a marching band was for.

"We're here," Alex said, confirming her suspicions.

She glanced at him. "What happens now?"

"You meet the king."

Great. If there was a survey at the end of this, she was going to mention Alex's lack of information as one of her complaints.

The limo door opened. Alex climbed out, then stepped aside so she could exit. Emma smoothed down the skirt she'd changed into on the plane and sucked in a breath for courage. It wasn't close to enough, so she wasn't surprised to find herself shaking as she stepped out in the warm afternoon.

Several people stood by the palace: Alex, the limo driver, a few uniformed men who could have been servants, but no one who looked like a king. So did royalty wait indoors for their visitors? Shouldn't Alex have briefed her on that sort of thing?

Before she could ask him, there was a movement to her left. Emma turned and saw a man step out of the shadows. He was tall, darkly handsome and almost familiar. Then the sun hit him full in the face and she gasped in stunned amazement. It couldn't be. Not after all this time. She'd thought... He would never...

The combination of shock, lack of sleep and food, and jet lag, conspired to increase her heart rate from nervous to hummingbird speed. The blood rushed from her head to her feet in two seconds flat. The world spun, blurred, then faded completely as she collapsed to the ground.

Prince Reyhan glanced at his father, the king of Bahania, and shook his head.

"That went well."

Chapter Two

Several servants rushed toward the fallen woman. Reyhan brushed them aside and crouched beside Emma. He took her wrist in his hand and felt her pulse.

Rapid, but steady.

"Call a doctor," he said firmly.

Someone went scuttling to do his bidding.

"She didn't hit her head," a young woman told him as she gently touched Emma's forehead. "I was watching as she fainted, Your Highness."

"Thank you. Are her rooms prepared?"

The woman nodded.

Reyhan gathered Emma into his arms. She lay limp, one hand pressing against his chest, the other dangling by her side. Her skin had paled and her breathing slowed.

He took a moment to study her long lashes and the fullness of her mouth. The thick, red hair he remembered hung in loose waves around her face. So much was the same, he thought. No doubt if he counted, he would find that there were still eleven freckles on her nose and cheeks.

How much had changed? Even as he silently asked the question, he found he didn't want to know. He rose and walked into the palace.

The king fell into step with him.

"At least she remembered you," his father said.

"Obviously with great joy."

"Perhaps she fainted with relief that you were to be together."

Reyhan didn't bother answering. Emma hadn't seen him in six years, and from what he'd been able to find out, she'd never made any attempt to get in touch with him. He had no idea what she recalled of their brief...relationship, but he doubted her fainting had anything to do with relief.

The guest quarters were on the second floor. Reyhan went directly there, wondering if his father would mention that other arrangements could have been made. Fortunately, the king remained silent.

Reyhan swept inside the suite of rooms he'd had prepared for Emma and set her on the sofa. A maid hovered in the corner.

"Find out when the doctor will arrive," he said.

The woman nodded and picked up a phone from the small table in the corner.

Reyhan returned his attention to Emma. She lay perfectly still. She hadn't moved at all while he'd carried her.

He sat next to her on the sofa and took her hand in his. Her fingers were cold. He brought them to his mouth and breathed on them.

"Emma," he murmured. "You must awaken."

She moved her head slightly and moaned.

"The doctor will be here in fifteen minutes," the maid told him.

"Thank you. A glass of water, please."

"Yes, Your Highness."

"Someone else could have carried her," the king said from the seat he'd taken across from the sofa. "Someone else can care for her now."

Reyhan narrowed his gaze. "No one touches my wife."

His father rose and crossed to the door. "It has been six years, Reyhan. Are you sure you still wish to claim the title of husband?"

Wish it or not, it was his. As was she.

Emma felt as if she were swimming against a very strong tide. But instead of water, she was trapped by air she had to push through to reach the surface. Thoughts formed and separated, her body felt heavy. Something had happened. She remembered that much. But what?

A cool, smooth surface pressed against her mouth as a strong, male voice demanded, "Drink this."

She parted her lips without considering refusing the request.

Water slipped into her mouth. She drank gratefully, then sighed when the glass was removed. Better, she thought, and opened her eyes.

Oh, my—it was him! Her eyes hadn't been playing tricks on her. She could feel the heat and strength of him as he sat next to her on the sofa. His hip pressed against her thigh. One of his hands held her own, while his dark gaze trapped her as neatly as a cage held a small bird.

Reyhan.

She wasn't sure if she said the name or merely thought it. Was it possible? After all these years?

She blinked and wondered if this was nothing more than a vivid dream. Only, her luck wasn't that good. No, the truth was he was real and she was in his presence, which didn't seem possible. It had been six years, she reminded herself again. Six years since he'd used her and tossed her aside. Six years since she'd hidden at her parents' house, crying for what could have been, secretly waiting for him to come and claim her, only to find out she'd waited in vain. He'd never come, and eventually she'd returned to her life—older, wiser and emotionally battered.

"So you return to us," he said, his low voice rumbling like distant thunder. "I don't remember you fainting before."

She bristled at the assumption that he *knew* things about her.

"I don't faint," she told him.

"Recent events suggest that you do. It was a long trip. Were you able to sleep at all?"

He spoke so casually, she thought in amazement.

As if nothing out of the ordinary had happened. As if it had been a few days rather than years since they were last together.

Outrage blossomed into fury. She wanted to yell at him, to scream or maybe even throw something. But years of being told that a lady didn't show her anger made it difficult for her to do more than glare.

Reyhan lightly touched her cheek. ''I see by the shadows under your eyes you did not sleep on the plane. At least not for long. Hardly a surprise, I suppose. You were not told why you were brought here. As I recall, you were always impatient and eager to find out things.''

Her attention split neatly between his words, which annoyed her, and the light stroking of his fingers against her skin. When his thumb grazed her lower lip, she was stunned by a jolt of awareness. The sensation cut through her like lightning, heating and melting everywhere it touched.

No! She would not react, she told herself. She wouldn't feel anything. She refused to. If this man really was Reyhan, then he filled her with nothing but contempt. He was beneath her notice.

One corner of his firm mouth turned up slightly. ''I see you want to spit at me like an ill-tempered kitten,'' he murmured. ''There is anger in your eyes.'' He glanced at her fingers. ''No claws. I doubt you can do much damage.''

Then he stunned her by kissing her knuckles.

She felt the warm brush of his mouth clear down to her toes. The hot, melting sensation grew until she wanted to purr like the kitten he'd mentioned. She thought about—

"Stop that right now," she said, snatching her hand back and folding her arms across her chest. The instruction was meant for both of them. In the past twenty-four hours, her world had taken a turn for the confusing, but she was determined to figure out what was going on. Which meant staying focused on the task at hand and not getting caught up in being in the same room as Reyhan.

She shifted away from him and pushed herself up into a sitting position. When he took hold of her arm to help her, she shook off his hand.

"I'm fine," she told him, her tone as icy as she could make it. "What I need from you is information. What is going on? What am I doing here? And while we're on the subject, what are *you* doing here?"

Before he could speak, there was a blur of movement, then a long-haired cream-colored cat with nearly violet eyes jumped up on her lap. She stared at it in amazement. Cats in the palace?

Reyhan grabbed the animal and set it back on the floor. The cat glared at him, gave a sniff of disgust and stalked off.

"Are you allergic to cats?" he asked.

"What? No."

"Good. The palace is filled with them. They are my father's."

His father? She rubbed her temple and tried to decide if she wanted to ask who his father was. While she would like the information, she was also afraid of it. Because crazy as it sounded, she had a feeling there was a better-than-even chance that Reyhan was somehow related to the king of Bahania.

Don't go there, she told herself as Reyhan held out the glass of water again. As she took it from him she found herself caught in his gaze.

She remembered his eyes most of all, she thought. How dark they were. How well they kept secrets. She'd once thought that if she could learn to read his eyes, she would know the man. But their few weeks together had not given them the time to learn very much about each other.

Sadness threatened. She tried to banish it by recalling what Reyhan had done to her—how he'd left and how she'd been alone and so afraid. Better to be angry. There was energy in anger and she had the feeling she was going to need it.

"I don't know what this game is," she told him, "but I'm not going to play. I wish to return home immediately. Please call Alex and have him take me back to the plane."

"Your escort from the State Department has already left the palace. He will spend the night at one of our most beautiful oceanside hotels, then fly back to your country in the morning." Reyhan dismissed the man with a flick of his wrist. "You will not see him again."

Anger faded as fear took its place. Alex was gone? So she was truly alone in the palace? Alone in this country?

Emma didn't know if she should try to bolt for freedom or bluff her way through. Her head was still spinning and she didn't look forward to trying to stand up, so that left bluffing. Something she'd never been very good at.

"What am I doing here?" she demanded. "Why did the king of Bahania ask me to come here for two weeks? And what are *you* doing here? You can't have anything to do with what's going on with me."

That last bit was more plea than forceful statement.

Reyhan stared at her. His strong, handsome features could have been set in stone—or steel—for all they gave away.

"Haven't you guessed?" he asked with quiet amusement, as if she were a child who had just performed the alphabet song flawlessly for the first time. "The king is my father, and the invitation is as much mine as his."

Her mind went blank. Completely and totally. It was like losing the lights during a thunderstorm.

The man next to her rose and squared his shoulders. Then he stared down at her with a haughty expression possibly honed through a lifetime of royal arrogance.

"I am Prince Reyhan, third oldest son of King Hassan of Bahania."

She blinked. Not possible, she told herself as some semicoherent thought process began in her brain. Not possible, not likely and she refused to believe it.

"A p-prince?" she asked, stumbling over the word.

No. No. No. Emma stared at the man standing in front of her. He couldn't be. A prince? Him? But they'd met at college. They'd dated. He'd taken her away with him and…hurt her dreadfully.

"The king decided it was time for me to marry,"

Reyhan told her. "There was no way I could agree to any match as I was already married. To you."

He kept on talking, but she wasn't listening. She couldn't. A prince? Married?

"But I…" She swallowed and tried again. "That wasn't real. Not any of it."

She remembered the quiet of the Caribbean island, the soft breezes, the lap of the ocean outside their hotel room. Reyhan had asked her to go away with him, and she'd agreed because she could refuse him nothing. At eighteen, she'd been more innocent than he'd realized. She'd been too ashamed to tell him she'd never dated before. He'd been her first, in every sense of the word.

Years later, when she'd looked back on the blur of hot days and long, endless nights, she'd comforted herself with the fact that she'd been too swept up in thinking she was in love to refuse Reyhan anything. She would never have considered asking him to go more slowly, to give her time to adjust. As for their marriage—her parents' lawyer had told her that had been a fake.

For a long time the realization had nearly destroyed her. She'd hated her weakness where he was concerned. Hated that she could still want him, even as he'd used and abandoned her. Time had healed her enough to give her perspective.

Reyhan's dark eyebrows drew together. "What wasn't real?"

"Our marriage. You just did that to get me into bed. Or get a green card."

As soon as she spoke the words, she realized she

might have made a mistake. Reyhan seemed to get bigger and taller as his temper grew. His anger was as tangible as the sofa she sat on, but a lot more frightening. His gaze narrowed and his mouth twisted into a disapproving and scornful line.

"A green card?" he asked, his voice thick with tension. "Why would I need that? I am Prince Reyhan. I am heir to the king of Bahania. I have no need to seek asylum elsewhere. This is my country."

He spoke proudly and with the confidence of who knew how many generations of royalty behind him.

"Yes, well." She cleared her throat. At the time, him wanting a green card had made sense. But now… "So that's not why you married me."

"It was not. I was in your country to continue my education. I earned my master's degree there." His expression turned contemptuous. "I honored you by giving you my name and my protection. As for trying to get you into my bed, the effort was hardly worth the meager reward."

She shrank back into the cushions. Humiliation joined the fear. As much as she tried to block out their nights together, they continued to haunt her. She supposed her part of it could be an illustration of what *not* to do on one's wedding night and the few nights that followed.

Not that it was her fault, she told herself, trying to grab on to a little temper to give her courage. She'd been the virgin. He should have done better, too.

But if Reyhan hadn't married her to get a green card or to sleep with her, why had he?

"Are you sure the marriage was real?" she asked. "My parents' lawyer said that it wasn't."

"Then their lawyer was mistaken." Reyhan glared at her. "You are my wife. That is why you were brought here. Now that you are in my country, in my home, you will treat me with respect and reverence. Is that understood?"

The need to bolt for freedom grew exponentially.

"Reyhan, I—"

But she never got to say whatever she'd been about to blurt out. For just at that moment, a petite, curvy, beautiful young woman walked into the room.

"This isn't good," the woman said. "I heard Emma had arrived and fainted at the sight of you. Is that true?"

Reyhan turned his attention from Emma to the woman. His glare only deepened.

The woman rolled her eyes. "Yeah, yeah, I know. You're insulted. But don't forget, I gave birth to your older brother's firstborn, so you have to be nice to me."

"One wonders what Sadik sees in you."

The woman leaned close and smiled. "I'm a hottie. It's a curse, but there we are."

Emma didn't think things could get more shocking, but she was proved wrong when Reyhan actually smiled at the woman, then kissed her forehead.

"Can you fix this?" he asked the woman.

"I'm not sure if you mean Emma or the situation. If you ask me, the one who needs fixing is you." She held up her hand before he could speak. "I'll do my best. I promise. Now why don't you give us some girl time together? I'll answer Emma's questions and make her feel at home. You can go work on your charm."

Reyhan raised his eyebrows. "I'm very charming."

"Uh-huh. Just a tip here. The 'I'm Prince Reyhan of Bahania' thing gets old really fast. Trust me. Sadik tried it on me, too."

"You're a troublemaker."

"That's true."

Reyhan nodded at Emma, then at the woman and left. Emma watched him go.

"Is this really happening?" she asked, feeling both weary and more confused than ever.

"It sure is," the other woman told her. "Right down to you sitting in the middle of the Bahanian royal palace." She plopped down next to Emma on the sofa and smiled. "Let's start at the beginning. Hi. I'm Cleo."

"I'm Emma. Emma Kennedy."

Cleo looked her over. "Love the hair. My sister-in-law Sabrina puts red highlights in hers, but the color is nothing like this. Is it real?"

It took Emma a second to process the question and realize Cleo wasn't asking about the hair itself, but the color.

"Yes, it's natural."

"Me, too," Cleo said, tugging on her short, spiky blond hair. "I put in gold highlights once, but was *that* a mistake. I thought I'd look more elegant and classy, which is so not going to happen. I'm stuck being a tacky bottle blonde for the rest of my life. No biggie. I mean I'm a princess, so now I can be royal and tacky, which I like.''

Emma felt as if she'd fallen into an alternate universe. "I'm sorry. I don't understand."

Cleo grinned. "I know. I'm rambling. Plus, do you really care about my hair? So here's the thing. You're in Bahania, and Reyhan really is a prince. There are four of them altogether. Murat is the oldest and heir to the throne. Then Sadik, my husband. He's in charge of finance. Reyhan is next. He runs the whole oil thing, and let me tell you, do they have a bunch of that floating around under the sand. Then Jefri, who is putting together a joint air force with El Bahar. There's also Zara, who was my foster sister and didn't know she was a princess until about a year ago, and Sabrina, the king's daughter. She lives in the desert, but that's a whole other story."

"Oh." Emma wasn't sure what to say. Her level of confusion had just gone off the scale. "That's a lot of people." She swallowed. "And you're Princess Cleo?"

"In the flesh." Cleo leaned close. "I'm from Spokane, Washington. That's right by Idaho. I know— not exactly the birthplace of a lot of royals. I had a ton to learn—protocol and how to address everyone. I've gotten involved with some charity work, which is pretty cool, and I have a new baby. Calah." Cleo's expression softened. "She's a dream. Just three months old."

Emma wanted to ask for note cards so she could write all this down and try to keep everyone and everything straight.

Reyhan, a Bahanian prince? Was it possible? And if he was, why had he married her?

"Do you know—" Emma cleared her throat. "There was a wedding a few years back. I thought maybe… My parents hired a lawyer and he thought it wasn't exactly real."

Cleo patted her arm. "Sorry. From what I've heard, it was plenty real. You're well and truly hitched to Reyhan. And he's just like his brother. All stuffy with an 'I'm the prince' attitude. That reverence and respect stuff. Oh, please. Okay, I'll do the respect thing, but reverence? It is *so* not going to happen."

So she was married. To a prince. *Her.*

"None of this makes sense," she whispered. "I don't understand."

Why had Reyhan done any of it? Why had he married her and disappeared from her life? And why, all of a sudden, did he pick now to get in touch with her? Did he want to marry someone else? The thought of it gave her an odd squeeze in her empty stomach, but still she had to know.

"Is he engaged?" she asked.

Cleo shook her head. "It's not like that. After Calah was born, the king decided it was time for Reyhan to tie the knot and give him more grandchildren. That's when he had to fess up about his relationship with you. That there was already a Mrs. Reyhan floating around."

Emma felt the room begin to fold around the edges. She had a feeling that if she'd been standing, she would have fallen again.

Cleo grabbed her hand. "Keep breathing," she instructed humorously. "I'm supposed to be making things better, not worse."

"It's not you," Emma told her. "It's everything. I can't believe what's happening."

"Hardly a surprise. The good news is, the palace is beautiful and Reyhan is pretty easy on the eyes, too. If you can get past all that honor and tradition, he has a wicked sense of humor. Won't that be nice?"

Nice? As in Emma would enjoy spending time with him? Was that the plan?

She shook her head. This wasn't happening, she told herself. None of it.

A tall man carrying a black case entered the room. Cleo waved a greeting.

"Dr. Johnson. You're still making house calls."

The older man smiled. "Yes, Princess Cleo. As I will continue to do."

Cleo leaned close to Emma. "Dr. Johnson is on call for the royal family. He's pretty cool. You'll like him."

Emma stared into the man's warm blue eyes and felt some of her anxiety fade.

He sat on the coffee table in front of her and reached for her hand. "How are you feeling? I heard you fainted."

"I don't know what happened," she admitted. "One second everything was fine, and the next, I was falling."

"Prince Reyhan filled me in on what occurred." He released her wrist. "Your pulse is normal. Have you blacked out since regaining consciousness?"

"No."

He glanced at Cleo. "Is she speaking coherently?"

"Yup. She's a little shell-shocked, but under the circumstances, who can blame her?"

Dr. Johnson made a noncommittal noise, then pulled out a stethoscope.

Fifteen minutes later he pronounced Emma exhausted, a little dehydrated, but otherwise fit. After giving her something to help her sleep, he said he would check on her the next day.

"Everything will be better in the morning," he promised as he left.

Emma watched him go, then nodded as Cleo excused herself to return to her baby. When Emma was finally alone, she stared around at the luxurious suite and the view of the ocean in the distance.

As much as she would like to believe Dr. Johnson, she had a feeling that the passage of night wasn't going to change one thing about her situation.

Reyhan did not want to speak with his father, but the request had been worded such that he'd known he didn't have a choice in the matter. So he'd appeared on time in the king's private rooms and now paced the length of the salon, all the while stepping to avoid the half-dozen or so cats milling around.

"What do you think now that you've seen her?" his father asked.

"That Emma should not have been brought here. A divorce could have been arranged without her presence."

"You defied me by marrying this young woman.

Six years have passed, and you never mentioned her
or spent time with her. I want to know why.''

Reyhan had no answers to the questions, nor did
he want to make up any. Thinking about Emma, being
with her... He reached the window and stared out at
the garden below. Seeing her again—it had been
worse than he'd imagined.

His father stood and crossed the room to stand next
to him. ''You are my son and a prince,'' he said. ''As
such, you were not permitted to take a wife without
my permission. Now it is done. Before I approve your
divorce, I will get to know this young woman. Two
weeks, Reyhan. Surely that is not too much to ask.''

Reyhan knew it was not. His father's request was
more than reasonable, and yet he would have given
much to keep Emma away.

He nodded once and walked to the door. ''Excuse
me, Father. My presence is required at a meeting.''

The king nodded, and Reyhan left.

As Reyhan walked toward the business wing of the
palace, he wondered how he would endure the next
fourteen days. There was much to occupy his time—
negotiations for oil purchases, dealing with a small
band of renegades, reviewing a list of potential brides.
Yet he knew none of that would fill his mind. Instead
he would think of a woman—the woman he had married. Emma. Their time apart had done nothing to
diminish his need for her. Six years ago she had been
his greatest weakness, and so she remained.

He paused at the door to his office. No one would
ever be permitted to know, he promised himself.
Wanting her, *needing* her, had nearly destroyed him

once before. That would not happen again. In two weeks the king would grant their divorce, she would be gone and he, Reyhan, would be allowed to remain strong. That he would live the rest of his life without her was of little consequence. He had survived this long. He would survive the rest of his days. Survive— not live. He reminded himself that most of the time, enduring was more than enough.

Chapter Three

Emma awoke to the not-so-surprising realization
that, despite the doctor's promise, little about her situation had changed or improved during the night. Not
that she'd expected either, although it would have
been nice.

She sat up in the huge bed and pulled her knees to
her chest. She remembered the doctor insisting she
take something to help her sleep, then she'd changed
into her nightgown and nearly collapsed into bed.
Then nothing.

The good news was she felt more rested. The bad
news...well, where exactly was she going to start?
There was so much to consider. That she might really
be married to Reyhan and might have been married

all this time. That she was in Bahania and he was the son of the king.

She shook her head. Way too many difficult thoughts for first thing in the morning. She should take a few minutes and get her bearings, then deal with the weirdness that was her life.

Emma rose. Her toes curled in the plush carpet that was thick enough to serve as a mattress in a pinch.

The bedroom had been decorated in pale yellows and blues. Ornate, carved dark wood furniture made up the elaborate headboard, footboard and matching nightstands. An armoire stood across the room. When she crossed to it she found a large television inside, along with a DVD player and a wide assortment of movies. There was also a detailed listing of the various channels available via satellite.

"Amazing," she murmured as she touched the carved birds and flowers on the door.

The bedroom itself was about the size of the average three-bedroom house back home in Dallas. She remembered the living room had been equally huge. With two parts anticipation and one part trepidation, she walked into the bathroom.

Huge didn't begin to describe it. Her entire apartment could have fit inside, with room to spare. The long marble vanity was about twice the length of her main kitchen counter. The tub had whirlpool jets and could have served as a playground for an entire water park full of seals. There was a glass-enclosed shower, towels as big as bedsheets and every toiletry known to womankind.

Emma turned in a slow circle and tried to imagine

what it would be like to live somewhere like this permanently. Was it possible to get used to this level of luxury, and would the palace continue to be a delight?

Twenty minutes later she'd showered and washed her face. After dressing, applying mascara and some lip gloss, she returned to the bedroom and put away the rest of her clothes. With that done, there was little to do but explore the rest of the suite and try to figure out what she was going to say when she next saw Reyhan.

In the light of day she knew that there was more to their relationship than her parents had told her six years ago when she'd returned home brokenhearted. But what exactly?

She left the bedroom and walked into the living room of the suite. The shutters were open and pulled back. The view was so amazing—blue ocean, bright sky, the tops of several trees—that she hadn't noticed Reyhan. But when she turned, she saw him seated at the dining room table in the corner. He studied the newspaper in front of him and hadn't seen her, either.

Her first thought was to bolt for the safety of her bedroom, but before she could get her feet to move, she found herself mesmerized by the man himself.

He was so handsome, she thought, remembering how his dark good looks had stunned her the first time they'd met. His hair was cropped short, in a stylish cut. Strong cheekbones emphasized the leanness of his features. His eyebrows were pulled together, giving him a stern expression. He looked intense and dangerous, something she remembered from their past together. Being around him had always left her tongue-tied and feeling more than a little foolish. That sensation returned big-time.

She winced as she recalled accusing him of marrying her to get a green card. He was a member of the Bahanian royal family. No doubt he could come or go at will just about anywhere in the world. As for wanting her in his bed…she had her doubts. The experience had been a disaster and after those first couple of nights, Reyhan had never come looking for her again.

"How long are you going to stand there?" he asked without looking up from his paper. "I have ordered you breakfast, Emma. You didn't eat before or after you arrived at the palace. I don't want you making yourself ill."

He set down the paper and looked at her. His dark gaze seemed to see all the way inside to her quivering heart. He raised one eyebrow.

"Are you so afraid of me? I swear that I have never attacked before ten or eleven in the morning. It is not civilized."

She glanced at the antique grandfather clock by the entryway. "So I'm safe for another ninety minutes?"

"At least."

He rose and pulled out a chair. Not knowing what else to do, she settled in it then watched as he lifted the tops off several serving dishes on the sideboard.

"What would you like?" he asked.

She blinked at him. "You're going to serve me?"

"You are my guest. In the interest of privacy I sent the maid away, so there is just the two of us this morning."

The implication being she was his responsibility? Reyhan had always had the most amazing manners. Apparently that hadn't changed.

She stood and crossed to the sideboard where she studied the assortment of offerings. There were eggs and bacon, fresh fruit, croissants, Danish and a selection of cereals, both hot and cold.

"I can't eat all this," she told him.

"I'll help." He motioned to the plates stacked on the left. "Please begin."

She reached for the plate. As she leaned forward, Reyhan moved and her hand grazed his arm. The instant heat nearly made her stumble. Awareness rippled along her skin like a sudden cool breeze, making her shiver and break out in goose bumps. She found herself wanting to touch him again, wanting to move closer, to have him touch her. Erotic images sprang into her mind, and before she knew what was happening, she realized it was difficult for her to catch her breath.

All of this happened in a matter of seconds. Then she became aware of herself, of Reyhan's expression of polite interest and she quickly stepped back and turned toward the food.

This was not good, she thought frantically. Not good at all. She didn't like how her heart raced whenever he was nearby. That hadn't happened before. If anything, he'd terrified her as much as he'd intrigued her. Not that she was any less terrified, it was just now she was frightened for a different reason.

She scooped fresh fruit onto her plate, along with some eggs. After taking a biscuit and butter, she returned to the table and poured them each coffee. Rey-han waited until she was seated before claiming his chair.

"You slept well?" he asked.

"Yes, thank you."

"Dr. Johnson said that your fainting was not likely to reoccur. He decided it was the combination of lack of food and sleep, along with minor dehydration and the shock of seeing me again." Reyhan's steady gaze never left her face. "Had I known you would react so strongly, I would have given you some warning. Stunning you into fainting wasn't my goal."

"Imagine what you could do if it was," she said lightly.

She noticed his single raised eyebrow again, but Emma refused to be intimidated, despite the instinct to cringe and apologize. She turned her attention to her breakfast instead and plunged her fork into a piece of mango. Sexual awareness swirled through the room like an erotic mist, but she was determined to ignore it.

Maybe she always had reacted so strongly to Rey-han but wasn't aware of it, she thought wryly. Maybe when they'd first met there had been this same powerful physical attraction between them but she'd been too young and innocent to recognize it. All she'd known back then was that she loved him and feared him with equal intensity. It was amazing she'd managed to find the strength to leave him.

Then she reminded herself that she hadn't left him. He'd left her and she'd hid out at her parents' home. Any additional contact had been through them. She hadn't even had the courage to tell him she didn't want to see him again. Not that he'd tried very hard.

"Why the heavy sigh?" he asked.

She looked up. "Did I sigh? I didn't mean to."

"You were thinking of the past."

"It's a logical place to go."

He nodded. "We will speak of it."

A statement or a command? "And if I don't want to?"

The words were out before she could stop them.

His mouth curved up in amusement. "You defy me?"

"Will that get me fifty lashes or time in the tower?"

"Nothing so boring." He sipped his coffee. "Why do you not wish to talk about our situation?"

"I do." She shrugged. "Knee-jerk reaction, I guess. My parents were always so protective. They meant well—they still do. My independence is hard-won and I get my back up when someone gives me orders."

"I see."

She had no idea what the silken words meant, nor did she want to ask for an explanation. She doubted whatever contact Reyhan had had with her parents had been especially pleasant.

"You're right," she said. "We need to talk about what happened and what's going to happen."

He nodded slightly. "If you wish."

"You're mocking me."

"I am terrified by your steely will."

Emma doubted anything terrified Reyhan. Which

meant he was teasing her. Interesting. She wouldn't have thought royal princes had senses of humor.

"Do you believe our marriage was real?" he asked.

"I don't want to, but, yes. You have no reason to lie, and my presence here is more than enough proof." She shifted in her seat. She'd been married for six years and hadn't known. Talk about being a fool.

"Why did you marry me?" she asked him, knowing it hadn't been for any of the usual reasons. At the time she'd thought Reyhan had loved her, but his behavior proved otherwise.

He chewed and swallowed. "You were a virgin," he said calmly. "I would not have defiled you."

Ten simple words that made her drop her fork, push back her chair and spring to her feet.

"What?" she demanded. "You married me to sleep with me? The whole thing was about sex?"

If love was out of the question, shouldn't he have at least liked her? Shouldn't he have pretended to care?

"Sit down, Emma. You're overreacting."

She took her seat before she remembered she wasn't going to let anyone run her life ever again. Once seated, it seemed silly to stand up and make a fuss. She settled on glaring at him.

Reyhan looked at her. "Why are you so outraged? Do you think there are any men who marry without the thought of their wives being a sexual partner?"

"Most men think about more than just doing it."

That made him get stiff and stern. His gaze narrowed. "I am Prince Reyhan of Bahania. When I married you, I not only gave you my name and protection, but honored you by making you a princess of my country. Had you been willing to continue our relationship, I would have brought you here where you would have lived in this palace. Neither you nor our children would have wanted for anything. I would have been faithful to you until I breathed my last breath. Who and what you are would have been passed along to our children, and through that, you would have joined in the history of my people. I believe that would be defined as more than just doing it.''

''But you never told me any of this,'' she reminded him, feeling more than a little embarrassed. ''Nor did you ask me if this is what I wanted with my life. What about my plans? My dreams? Marrying you could have changed my world forever.''

''Is that such a bad thing?''

She thought of her small apartment and her quiet life. She remembered her conversation with Cleo the previous night and what she'd said about the palace and the princes.

''You didn't give me a choice,'' she said. ''Not about staying or going. You married me without telling me the truth, then you disappeared without a word.''

Reyhan leaned back in his chair. ''Our recollection of the events that happened are very different, but that is of no consequence. What matters is our present circumstances. We are married—something neither of us wishes to continue. The king's permission is required for a prince to divorce, and he has insisted you spend two weeks here until he will grant the decree.''

Countless years of having her life run by her parents had made Emma hypersensitive to being told what to do. Her first instinct was to tell Reyhan that maybe she didn't want a divorce, thank you very much. Maybe she wanted to stay married.

She stopped herself before she could blurt out the irrational statement. She didn't know the man. She didn't want anything to do with him. Of course she wanted to go get a divorce and go back to her life.

''You didn't need his permission to get married, but you need it for a divorce,'' she said. ''That doesn't make sense.''

''I did need his permission to marry. I defied him.''

Simple words, she thought, but stunning. He'd defied the king? To marry her? Which brought her back to her original question—why?

For sex? He was a handsome, wealthy, royal guy. Couldn't he get any woman he wanted? So why her?

She had a feeling that the earth would stop turning before she found out the answer to that one, so she chose another topic of conversation.

''So after the divorce you'll marry someone else.'' A thought occurred to her. ''Have you already chosen your new bride?'' Cleo had said he wasn't engaged, but was he already in love?

Reyhan shook his head. ''My marriage will be arranged.''

Emma blinked at him. ''You mean she'll be picked by someone else? What if you don't like her?''

He shrugged. ''That is of little consequence.''

It felt like a really big consequence to her.

"But she could make you crazy."

"Then we will have little contact. My duty is to produce heirs for the kingdom. I will not turn my back on my responsibility."

He had a duty? But where had all that duty been when he'd married her? And why would he agree to a wife he might not even like?

"Do you get to spend time with the potential brides in advance? Like *The Bachelor* for royalty?"

"No."

"But—"

He rose, cutting her off. "I have a meeting," he said politely. "Please think of your time here in Bahania as a vacation. In two weeks you can return to Texas as if nothing ever happened. In the meantime, if you need anything, please ask one of the servants. You are an honored guest of the king."

With that he nodded and left.

Emma stared after him. She might be going home, but she doubted she would ever forget what had happened here. In a matter of hours, her world had turned upside down.

She rose and crossed to the French doors that led to a beautiful balcony. When she stepped outside, she saw the balcony stretched the length of the palace, perhaps even circling around it. A nice place to take a walk, she thought as she moved to the carved railing and leaned down to inspect the wonderful gardens below.

Stone paths meandered through what looked like a

formal English garden. A fountain gurgled, while birds sang from nearby trees.

Hardly what she'd expected for a desert nation, she thought, then remembered the desalinization plant Alex had pointed out on their drive from the airport. Bahania created much of the fresh water her people used. Interesting, but hardly what was on her mind.

She turned her attention from the garden to her left hand. Reyhan had placed a simple gold band there after the ceremony. He'd kissed her and promised to replace it with any ring she would like. At the time she'd thought he'd been caught up in the romance of the moment, making promises he could never keep. Now she knew he'd been telling the truth.

But why hadn't he told her the rest of it? About him being the prince and that he'd always planned to return there? And why hadn't her parents been able to find out that she was really married? Who had told them the ceremony had been a sham and why hadn't they questioned the information?

Would it have made a difference? After the fact, she could say yes. But at the time? She'd been hurt and afraid and not that interested in being Reyhan's wife. Their few days together as husband and wife had been spent in bed. He had wanted her with a passion that had terrified and confused her. While she hadn't minded him touching her, she hadn't much liked it, either. He'd been too intense, too hungry, too everything.

Now the thought of those dark eyes gazing at her with unmistakable desire made her breathing quicken. Which so did not make sense. She had no reason to be attracted to Reyhan. She barely knew him. She wasn't even sure she liked him. So why was she anticipating the next time she saw him?

Reyhan walked from the residential wing of the palace toward the business wing, moving quickly but with his thoughts still outpacing his steps.

There wasn't a part of him that was not on fire with desire for Emma. He needed her as he needed the wide spaces of the desert. She was as much a part of him, and yet as out of reach as the stars.

If only he'd been able to keep her from coming to Bahania. But his father had insisted on meeting the woman Reyhan had married and then left behind. Royal pronouncements could only be avoided for so long, and in the end he had run out of excuses. So Emma was here—haunting him. He wanted her with a grim desperation that threatened his world, and he could not have her. Not before and not now. She was, he acknowledged, the one woman on earth who could bring him to his knees. Him—a prince. A man of power and action. If she knew how he really felt…

He reminded himself she did not know, nor would she be affected if she did. She'd made her feelings clear six years ago and there was no reason to think they would have changed.

Only twelve more days, he told himself. He could survive that, especially if he avoided her.

He reached the business wing and asked his assistant to come into his office. When the young man was seated, Reyhan pulled out his schedule. He was about to find himself very, very busy.

* * *

Emma restlessly wandered around the suite. She might be an honored guest of the king, but she wasn't sure what that meant in terms of what she could and could not do. Were there self-guided tours of the palace? The maid had disappeared and she didn't know who else to ask. The last thing she wanted was to wander into some forbidden room and find herself at the wrong end of a pointy sword.

She stared at the phone and wondered what would happen if she picked it up. Did the palace have an operator? In movies, the White House always did, and the palace was at least twice as big. Wasn't an operator required?

A knock on the suite's main door saved her from finding out. For a split second, her heart fluttered in anticipation. Reyhan? Had his meeting ended early and had he decided to return to speak with her? Had…

She pulled open the door and tried not to look disappointed when she saw Cleo standing there. The petite blonde had a baby in her arms.

"Remember me?" Cleo asked. "We met last night."

"Of course," Emma said with a smile. "You came to rescue me."

Cleo grinned. "Someone had to. These princes," she said, shaking her head. "They have no idea how intimidating they can be, and between you and me, we can't ever let them know."

She walked into the suite and held out her daughter. "This is Calah. I'm going to say 'Isn't she beautiful?'"

and I really need you to agree with me. I know, I know. Every mother thinks her baby is beautiful. I hate being a cliché, but there it is.''

Emma glanced at the sleeping baby. ''She *is* beautiful. You and your husband are going to have to beat boys off with a stick.''

''I suspect Sadik will just glare menacingly and that will be enough.'' Cleo plopped down on the sofa and held out the baby. ''Are you a cuddler or do infants make you uneasy?''

Emma sat next to her and took Calah in her arms. ''I love holding babies. I'm a delivery room nurse so I'm around newborns all the time. It's a great specialty and I love it, but every now and then I get the urge to move to pediatrics.''

Cleo's eyebrows arched. ''Ah, so you love children. Does Reyhan know?''

''I don't think so.'' The information would hardly matter. He might want heirs but not with her.

''Interesting. So tell me everything about your life.''

Emma gently rocked the baby and breathed in the sweet scent of her. ''There's not much to tell. I'm a nurse, I live in Dallas and now I'm here. But what about you? How did you come to be here, and married to a prince?''

Cleo drew her feet up and leaned back against the sofa. ''Well, I already told you I'm from Spokane. I grew up dirt-poor and without much family. Eventually I went into the foster care system, which turned out to be a good thing because I got to meet Zara. She was the daughter of the woman who took me in.

Anyway, we became good friends, then practically sisters. Years after her mother had died, Zara went through her things and found these letters to her mother from the king of Bahania.''

Emma stared at her. ''You're kidding.''

''Nope. He'd met her when she'd been a dancer and he'd fallen for her big-time. Apparently theirs was a great love, but Zara's mom knew it would never last so she bailed without telling him.''

''How sad,'' Emma said.

''I agree. I mean she could have *tried* to make it work. Anyway, Zara found the letters and the two of us headed over here to see if the king really was her father. And he was.''

''That must have been a shock for both of them.''

''It was. I mean violà, instant princess. She also met Rafe, who is American but also a sheik, and she married him—but that is a more complicated story.''

Emma laughed. ''Oh, right. Because this one isn't. So you stayed with Zara and then married Prince Sadik?''

''Not exactly. He and I—well, it was sort of spontaneous combustion. But he was a prince and I worked at a copy store. I mean until I'd come to Bahania I'd never been anywhere. I knew I wasn't princess material. So I went home. But I had to come back for Zara's wedding to Rafe, and I was pregnant and I didn't want anyone to know. The king found out, then Sadik, then we got married, but he wouldn't admit he loved me and it was horrible, but he came to his senses and now we're blissfully happy.''

Emma didn't know what to say. "That's an amazing story."

Cleo grinned. "I know. I can't wait until Calah is old enough to hear the romantic bits. I won't tell her about getting pregnant or anything." Her eyes widened. "Oh, I should warn you. Both Zara and Sabrina are pregnant. I think there's something in the water, so don't drink anything but bottled." She glanced at her daughter. "Unless you want one of your own."

Emma was dealing with enough changes right now, although a child... She shook off the thought. No point in going there. Not now.

"I don't think this is a good time for me," she said. "Plus there's the whole needing-a-man thing."

"Is this where I point out that you have a husband?"

One who had made it plain he'd found her anything but interesting in bed? "No, thanks."

Cleo nodded. "I understand. But that doesn't mean I won't think it. So how did you and Reyhan meet?"

"It was at college. My first semester." Those days felt like a lifetime ago. "I was a brand-new freshman—technically an adult, but not emotionally. Not even close." She shrugged. "I'm the only child of older parents. They'd given up on ever having children when I came along. I was a surprise, but a happy one. My parents were so thrilled, they were determined to keep me safe no matter what. Which meant keeping me sheltered. It took my entire senior year of high school to convince them to let me go to a college that required me living a couple hundred miles away."

"Reyhan's older, right?" Cleo asked. "You couldn't have had a class together."

"We didn't. I was socially backward, and I would never have had the courage to talk to an actual man. I was walking home from the library when a couple of drunk guys started hassling me. I'm sure it was harmless, but I was too inexperienced to know what to do. I panicked and started pleading with them, which they found pretty funny. I was terrified and took off running. I ran smack into Reyhan. My books went flying, I'm sure I screamed and it was a mess. By the time it was sorted out, the guys were long gone and I was convinced Reyhan had rescued me from certain death."

Cleo sighed. "That sounds romantic."

Emma hadn't thought of it in that way. "I thought he was handsome and mysterious. Very attractive, of course. I was stunned when he asked me out." She shifted the baby, taking more of her weight on her lap.

"But you said yes."

"Would you have said anything else?"

"Probably not. The rescue would be really tough to ignore. It's very princely." She laughed. "I say that so calmly, but I'm used to Sadik being royal now. At the beginning it was a big deal to me."

"Do you miss your old life?"

"Not even for a minute. Not just because this is so much nicer—which it is. But because of Sadik. I love him." Her dark blue eyes glowed with affection. "He makes me insane, but that's okay. I drive him crazy, too. Besides, being different keeps things interesting.

And he loves me.'' She glanced at Emma. ''Handsome, arrogant prince types may be hard to tame, but when they love, it's with every part of themselves.''

Emma fought against a surge of envy. She had always wanted to be loved like that by a man. It wasn't that her parents hadn't cared for her, they had. But their love had been about protecting her from a difficult and frightening world. She'd always wanted just to be loved for herself.

Cleo shrugged. ''Okay, I get carried away. That's part of my charm. So enough about me and my past. Are you excited about living in the palace?''

''It should be an interesting vacation. At least that's how I'm trying to look at it.''

''Your one chance to be a princess?''

''Something like that.''

Cleo grinned. ''What if you find you like it so much, you want to stay?''

''Not an option. As soon as my two weeks are up, I'm heading back to Dallas.'' And her regularly scheduled life. There was nothing for her here in Bahania. She ignored the little voice inside that whispered there wasn't much for her back in Dallas, either.

Chapter Four

Reyhan had hoped the large palace would provide enough room for him to avoid Emma, but he had not taken his father's need to meddle into account. Now that the king had passed control of much of the day-to-day details of the country on to his sons, he had far too much free time to plan ways to torment them. His newest strategy began with an invitation for both Reyhan and Emma to join him for dinner.

Reyhan studied the casually worded e-mail and knew the phrase "if it's convenient" was there for show. Should Reyhan protest it was not convenient, his father would change the request to an order. Defying one's father was easily accomplished. Refusing the king was another matter, especially when Reyhan needed the monarch's agreement to the divorce.

Which was why he found himself walking toward his father's private quarters that evening, trying not to think about how he would survive several hours in Emma's company.

Before she had arrived, he had nearly convinced himself that everything was different. That he no longer had feelings for her, and even if he did, that she was not the same woman. But a few minutes with her had told him that not only did she still have that ultimate power over him, she had somehow retained the gentle sweetness that had first drawn him to her.

When he reached his father's suite, he squared his shoulders. He was Prince Reyhan of Bahania. Royal, powerful and without weakness. He would survive this meeting and any others. He would endure and in the end, Emma would be out of his life forever.

"My son," his father said happily as Reyhan walked into the main salon. "How good to see you."

"And you, my father."

The king's cheer warned Reyhan that his father might have a trick or two coming during the dinner and that he would be wise to stay alert.

He crossed to the wet bar and poured himself a Scotch, then walked to the large sofa facing the French doors leading to the balcony. Only one cat lay on a center cushion. Reyhan avoided it as he sat down.

"Emma should be here shortly," his father said, stroking the large Persian draped across his lap.

Reyhan had offered to escort her himself, but the king had said he preferred to speak with his son privately first. Now Reyhan waited patiently.

"Your wife is a very pretty young woman," his father said.

Reyhan nodded. He never thought of Emma as "his wife." If he had, he would have claimed her, despite her wishes to be as far away from him as possible. He would have wanted to have her, take her, *be* with her. It had been safer for them both to be on opposite sides of the planet. Literally. He'd forced himself to think of her only on rare occasions, usually at night, when he couldn't sleep and the sounds of the Arabian Sea had echoed with her soft voice.

"I arranged tonight's dinner so I could get to know her," his father said.

Reyhan didn't like the sound of that. "She will be leaving in a few days."

"Until then, she is my daughter-in-law. A relationship of some importance."

Reyhan wasn't sure if his father meant that or was trying to make trouble. On the king's side was his close ties with Cleo, Sadik's wife. She was a favorite and spent much time in the king's company. If that happened with Emma, as well, his father might not want to agree to the divorce. Reyhan knew he could not stay married. Not to her. Not with his need burning so hotly inside.

Before he could come up with a reason to keep them apart, there was a knock at the main door. He rose, bracing himself for the impact of seeing her again.

"Come in," the king called.

A young woman pushed opened the door, entered

and bowed her head. Emma followed her, pausing uncertainly just past her escort.

Reyhan set down his drink, then crossed to her. As he approached, he took in the emerald-green sheath that clung to her sensual curves, the elegant upswept way she'd styled her dark red hair and the makeup emphasizing her eyes and mouth. She needed no artifice to make her more beautiful, yet he appreciated the effort…and the results.

Wanting flared, as did heat. He ignored both, concentrating instead on the excitement and apprehension battling in Emma's green eyes. A tentative smile tugged on the corners of her mouth, as if she wasn't sure which emotion would win.

When he stopped beside her, he reached for her hand. The second his fingers closed around hers, the ache inside of him increased to unbearable. Still, he dismissed the painful need and settled her small hand in the crook of his arm. He urged her toward his father, who had put down the cat and risen.

"Father, this is Princess Emma, my wife. Emma, this is King Hassan of Bahania."

He felt her stiffen at "Princess" and wondered if she'd considered her position here. As long as they were married, she was a member of the royal family. Bahania was a long way from her life in Texas.

"Enchanted," the older man said as he took her free hand and lightly kissed the back of it. "Would you like something to drink? Champagne? We should toast the moment."

"No. I—I'm fine."

The king drew her from Reyhan and settled her on

the sofa, next to the sleeping Siamese. He took the opposite side of the couch, leaving Reyhan the chair.

Not difficult duty, Reyhan thought as he sat. Emma was in his direct line of vision. He could visually trace her profile, the line of her neck, the length of her bare arms. And while looking at her, he could remember their few nights together. How she'd felt when he'd touched her. How she'd tasted when he'd kissed her. The tight dampness of her virgin body when he'd first claimed her as his own.

The images had an expected result, and he was forced to shift slightly in his chair. Stop, he ordered himself. Thinking about what had been once and never would be again offered torment but little else.

"Tell me about yourself," the king said. "You are from Texas?"

Emma nodded. "The Dallas area. I've lived there nearly all my life. Except when I was at college."

"Do you have brothers and sisters?"

"No. My parents had actually given up on ever having children when I came along." She smiled. "I was a surprise."

The sweet pull of her lips hit Reyhan like a punch in the gut. He consciously relaxed his muscles and sucked in a breath. Soon she would be gone and then he could forget she had ever lived, he told himself.

"A happy one," his father said.

Emma laughed. "You're right. My parents have made it very clear how much they adore me." Her humor faded slightly. "They are extremely protective."

"As they should be. A daughter such as yourself is a rare treasure."

"Thank you," she murmured as she bowed her head.

Reyhan caught the light flush on her cheek. So she still blushed. When he had first met her it seemed that everything he did caused her to blush. A compliment, a kiss, a whisper of desire. She had been the most innocent woman he'd ever met.

"Treasure or not, they made it difficult to have a life," she said. "Not that I don't love them dearly. But there were things I wanted to do." Her voice had turned wistful. "They were very strict about things like school dances and dating."

His father raised his eyebrows. Reyhan stepped into the conversation.

"Many Western high schools offer chaperoned dances for the students," he said.

"A dangerous practice," the king said. "Now you know why I sent you to England for much of your education."

"An all-boys school," Reyhan said dryly. "It was thrilling."

Emma glanced at him and smiled. For that second, there was a connection between them. He could nearly see the sparks arcing across the room and feel the temperature increasing.

"Where did you meet my son?" the king asked, breaking the spell.

Emma returned her attention to the monarch. "At college. It was my first year there. I'd had to beg my parents to let me go. I was very excited, but scared, too.''

''And did he sweep you off your feet?''

She swallowed, blushed, then nodded. ''Yes. He was very charming. Very…worldly.''

Reyhan thought of the young man he'd been at twenty-four. Hardly worldly, except in Emma's inexperienced view. He'd wanted her and he'd pursued her with a single-minded focus that had left her nowhere to escape. He'd been determined to have her, and, upon discovering she was a virgin, he'd married her.

''Yours was a brief courtship,'' the king said.

Emma glanced at Reyhan. ''I…we…''

''She knew nothing of who I was,'' Reyhan said, interrupting her hesitation. ''I alone defied you, Father. The blame, the responsibility, is mine.''

Emma's eyes widened slightly, but she didn't say anything. The king nodded.

''You stayed together only a short time.'' The king's words were more statement than question.

''You know this,'' Reyhan said as he stepped in again. ''I was called home because of Sheza's death.'' He glanced at Emma. ''My aunt.''

''But you did not return to your wife.''

He had tried, Reyhan thought bitterly. He had called and attempted to see her, but she refused to have anything to do with him. Eventually her father had ordered him to stay away. No explanation save that Emma regretted the marriage and never wanted to see him again.

He'd told himself the sting he'd felt was little more

than wounded pride. That he hadn't actually cared about her. Loved her.

He shrugged with a casualness he didn't feel. "The past is finished. What value is there in discussing it now?"

"I wish to know," his father said. He looked at Emma. "So after things did not work out with Reyhan, you returned to your parents?"

Reyhan didn't save her from that probing question mostly because he wanted to hear her answer.

"I, ah, stayed with them until the new semester started, then I returned to college. By then, Reyhan was gone."

True enough. Once he'd realized he'd lost her, he'd finished the requirements for his master's and had gone back to Bahania. He'd never tried to see Emma again.

"And what do you do now?" the king asked. "How do you spend your days?"

Emma looked confused, as if she expected them to already know this. "I'm a delivery room nurse. I received my RN and went to work in a Dallas hospital." She shifted in her seat and smiled. "It wasn't easy, let me tell you. My parents really hated the idea of me living on my own, but I knew it was time. I have a good job. I can support myself."

Reyhan stiffened. "You what?"

His father glared at him. "You abandoned your responsibility?"

"I did not." He turned to Emma. He wasn't surprised that she worked. Many women preferred to fill their day with a job, especially when there weren't small children to tend to. But that she acted as if she *needed* the money. "You do not need to work to support yourself."

She stared at him. "Excuse me? How would you know what I need and don't need?"

"I left you financially provided for."

Emma leaned back in the sofa, trying to put a little distance between herself and an obviously furious Reyhan. She wouldn't mind his temper so much if she knew what he was so mad about. Nothing made sense. He hadn't left her a dime.

"You didn't do anything when you left," she said, then winced when he seemed to puff up and get even madder.

"After we were married, I opened a checking account for your personal use. Two hundred and fifty thousand dollars were put in a checking account. When the balance reached below a hundred thousand, the account was to be replenished."

Two hundred and fifty *thousand* dollars? He'd left her money?

"I don't understand," she whispered.

"What is complicated about the information?"

Good point, she thought. But her head was spinning and nothing made sense. "Why would you take care of me?"

Wrong question, she thought as he stiffened even more.

"I am Prince Reyhan of Bahania and you are my wife. You are my responsibility. When you did not use the money, I assumed it was out of pride and anger. I sent a letter requesting you reconsider, and then funds were withdrawn, as they have been ever since.''

Now it was her turn to get all huffy. "Wait a minute. I didn't know about any money and I sure didn't spend it.''

"You knew. When you refused to see me, I spoke with your father. I gave him the account information.''

Her father? "You came to see me?''

"Of course.''

No. That's not how it happened. Emma distinctly remembered being curled up on her bed back in her parents' house, praying for Reyhan to contact her. But he never had. Not a note, not a phone call and certainly not a visit.

Unless he'd shown up while she'd been…ill.

"I was sick for a while,'' she said, telling herself it wasn't exactly a lie. There'd been a sickness of spirit.

"I came by several times, in fact.''

Had he? Was it possible her parents had kept the information from her?

She thought they might not have wanted to tell her that Reyhan had been by to see her, but they never would have kept information about that kind of money from her. They loved her. They were devoted to her.

"I don't believe you,'' she said. "Not about the money. If I don't know about it, who withdrew funds? Not my parents. They would never do that. This doesn't make sense. You disappeared from my life for six years, only to drag me over here and tell me you want a divorce. Why should I believe anything you say?''

"Because I do not lie."

She glanced at the king, but he seemed more amused than upset by the argument. Which was fine. She was upset enough for two people. She turned back to Reyhan. "Liar or not, you've insulted my parents and for no good reason. I don't know what this game is, but I'm done playing it."

She stood and walked out of the room.

After fifty feet down the hall she had the unsettling thought that it was probably considered a very bad thing to walk out on the king of Bahania. She paused, not sure if she should go back and apologize, or keep going. Before she could decide, she heard footsteps, then Reyhan rounded the corner and stopped in front of her.

He was obviously furious—tight-lipped and hard-eyed. Without speaking, he took her by the arm and led her away. She didn't recognize the twists and turns they took, even when they ended up in front of her suite. Reyhan opened the door and hustled her inside.

When he released her, she had the strangest urge not to move away. For a split second she thought about throwing herself into his arms and begging him to hold her. As if his embrace would make things right.

Not in this universe, she thought, taking a step back and bracing herself for whatever he had to say.

His gaze narrowed. "Why do you question what I tell you?''

"Why shouldn't I?"

"Because there is proof of everything. For weeks I kept vigil outside of your parents' home. I called or came by every day. I returned to claim you as my wife only to be told you refused to see me. I left when I received your letter."

Emma didn't understand any of this. "What letter?"

"The one you wrote telling me you regretted meeting me and everything about our marriage and that you only wanted me to disappear."

He spoke stiffly, as if the words were difficult to say.

"That's crazy," she told him. "I never wrote that."

She hadn't thought it, either. Not at the time. She'd longed to see Reyhan, but he'd abandoned her.

"You used me," she continued. "I don't know why, but you got it in your head you wanted to sleep with me, so you pretended to care about me." She couldn't say the word *love,* not even now. "You took advantage of me for a long weekend, then took off. No explanation, nothing."

It took a lot to get her angry, but once she was on a roll, she liked to keep going. She remembered the pain and humiliation of being tossed aside like a broken toy.

"You promised me things," she said, her voice rising. "You talked about our life together and I believed you. I trusted you and you just took what you wanted and walked away."

"I left because a beloved aunt died."

"Did the funeral take six weeks to prepare? Did you ever once call me? Did you think to tell me what was going on?"

He frowned. "Of course. I phoned nearly every day."

She rolled her eyes. "Oh, right. And I just happened to be out."

"That is what I was told."

She turned her back on him and walked to the floor-to-ceiling glass wall. None of this mattered, she told herself, trying to cool her temper. Soon it would be behind her. She had to remember the big picture.

Reyhan spoke into the silence. "If you think so little of men, you must be pleased to be rid of me. Just a few more days and the marriage will be over. As if it had never existed."

Fury surged. "Right. Because you can dismiss what happened. Because it didn't matter." She spun back to face it. "It mattered to me. Do you have any idea how innocent I was? I'd barely kissed one boy in high school. And then there was you. You didn't just seduce me, Reyhan, you took what you wanted, without regard for my feelings. I'll never forgive that."

His expression turned menacing. "You were more than willing."

"I was terrified. Now I'd know better. Now I'd tell you no."

"Are you saying I had you against your will?"

He hadn't, not exactly, but she was mad. "Yes."

"You were a child, only interested in chaste kisses

and expensive presents. A child who couldn't please a man.''

That hurt. She tried not to remember how embarrassed she'd been, how awkward and unsure.

"You were a man who couldn't be bothered with seducing his bride. Instead you just took.''

They were both enraged, breathing hard and glaring at each other. A part of her was terrified, but she refused to back down. Not even when he moved closer still. Not even when he reached behind her and grabbed her by the hair and pulled her up against him.

"If that is who I am," he said with frighteningly soft menace, "a liar and a defiler of women, then there is no point in holding back now.''

He kissed her. Not the soft kiss of seduction or coaxing, but a kiss of power. He was a man with something to prove. His firm lips pressed hard against her own, claiming her with passion.

She wanted to protest, to scream, to pull back, but she could not. They touched everywhere. Her body pressed against his, their legs tangled. She put up her hands to push him away, but when her palms brushed against the hard planes of his suit-covered chest, she found herself unable to protest…or even breathe.

Fire consumed her. Hot and hungry, it swept through her, melting her resolve, her reason. Against her will, she found herself moving her hands from his chest to his shoulders. She clung to him because letting go would mean collapsing at his feet. Worse, she kissed him back.

She couldn't explain it, and given the choice, she would probably deny it, but there it was. A need that grew. Wanting was alive inside of her. In that moment, with his mouth against hers and his hands moving from the back of her head to her shoulders, then to her hips, she couldn't get close enough.

Emma wanted to surrender, to crawl inside of him. When his kiss gentled and he stroked her lower lip with his tongue, she parted for him and anticipated his more intimate kiss.

At the first stroke of his tongue against her own it was all she could do not to scream. At the second, she ceased to have a will of her own. And with the third, she clamped her lips around him, greedily holding him in place, wanting him to kiss her forever.

She ached. Her breasts, between her legs, all over. Her skin felt hot and too tight. She wanted to strip her dress off and have him touch her everywhere. She wanted to be naked, vulnerable, offering herself to him.

She rubbed one hand against the back of his neck. He held on to her hips and then dropped his hands to her rear where he squeezed the curves. She surged against him, wanting to rub like a lonely cat. But before she could put her plan into action he broke the kiss and stepped away.

They stared at each other. Loud breathing filled the silence. Emma was pleased to note that Reyhan looked as swept away by passion as she felt.

Perhaps they should call a truce, she thought. Start over as friends. Friends who could bring about the end of the world with just a kiss.

''You have learned much in my absence,'' Reyhan said, his cold voice contrasting with the fire in his eyes. "Before you accuse me of more sins, you should look at yourself. A wife who takes lovers. Isn't there a name for that?"

Her mouth dropped open, but before she could snap back at him, he was gone.

Emma glared at the shut door and yelped in anger and frustration.

"That is not fair!" she yelled into the empty room. "I didn't know we were married and you know it."

Besides, there hadn't been any other men. Not seriously. And she'd never allowed any of them into her bed. If she kissed better now, it was because she was older, and because kissing Reyhan had made her feel things she'd never felt before. Not even *with* him.

Emma slowed her breathing and tried to calm down. She was shaking and not just because she was mad. She was shaking in reaction to what had happened when Reyhan had kissed her. She'd wanted him. Funny how she'd started to worry that there was something wrong with her because none of the guys she went out with had made her want to get naked and do the wild thing. Just her luck that the first one to push all her buttons was an arrogant prince who just happened to be a man trying to get her out of his life as quickly as possible.

"I don't think I can handle any more," she said quietly as she stepped out onto the balcony. "By the time I get home, I'm going to need a serious vacation."

She crossed to the railing and glanced down into the beautiful gardens. The peaceful setting began to ease her tension and she felt herself relaxing. After a time, she heard voices and searched until she found a couple walking into the gardens.

Even from two stories above, she recognized Cleo. The tall, handsome man at her side must be her husband. Emma couldn't make out the words, but she heard the affection in their voices. Sadik turned to his wife and held out his arms. Cleo willingly stepped into his embrace and they kissed.

Not wanting to intrude on an obviously private moment, Emma stepped back and returned to her suite. Alone in the silence, she paced the length of the living room as she tried to figure out what happened next.

Should she say anything to Reyhan? To the king? Could she just leave?

The musical chimes of a grandfather clock caught her attention. She stared at the face and calculated the time difference with Texas, then crossed to the telephone and pressed zero, hoping to get an operator. Less than a minute later, she heard her mother's voice on the phone.

"Emma! How lovely to hear from you. Where are you, darling? George, it's Emma. Pick up the other phone."

Emma waited until she heard her father's familiar "Hello, kitten," before sighing in relief. The tension fled her body and for the first time in three days she knew everything was going to be all right.

"Are you enjoying your vacation?" her mother asked. "I've heard spring in San Francisco is very beautiful. Are you getting a lot of fog?"

Emma winced as she remembered the lie she'd told her parents. Alex from the State Department had made the suggestion and she'd gone along. Now she wondered if the original idea had been Reyhan's.

"I'm not in San Francisco," she told them.

"What?" Her father's voice turned worried. "Was there a problem with the plane? Do you need us to come and get you?"

"No. I'm fine. I'm in Bahania."

"The Bahamas?" her mother asked.

"No. Bahania. It's next to El Bahar. In the Middle East. I'm here because of Reyhan."

Her mother gasped. "I knew that horrible man wouldn't stay gone. Oh, George, he kidnapped her. We have to call the police. They'll know what to do."

"Now, Janice. Don't jump to conclusions. Kitten, are you all right? Did he hurt you?"

"No, Daddy. Reyhan has been very polite." She had no intention of mentioning the kiss they'd just shared. "Why did you say you didn't think he wouldn't stay away, Mom? You told me he never bothered to come see me."

There was a long silence. Finally her father spoke. "He might have stopped by a time or two."

Deep in her heart Emma wasn't surprised. Her parents loved her and wanted to protect her from everything. That would include what they saw as a dangerous man intent on using their daughter. The problem with them admitting guilt in one area was that now she had to doubt them about everything, involving her pseudomarriage and the time following it.

"Just come home," her mother pleaded. "Emma, you don't belong there with those people. We'll come get you if you like. Wouldn't that be nice? Then we could all go to Galveston together. I'll bet that nice house we used to rent is available. It's not too close to summer. I could call and check and we could—"

"Mom, no. I'm not coming home just yet and I don't want you to come get me. I'm fine. I'm just..." How to explain what she was doing?

"That man is going to bewitch you," her mother said. "Just like he did before. It's not right. He should be in jail."

"For what?" Emma asked. "He married me and provided for me." Sadness overwhelmed her. Sadness for what had happened and what she'd believed. Sadness that her parents couldn't have believed in her enough to tell the truth.

"He abandoned you," her father pointed out. "What kind of man does that? He tried to turn your head, the way he's doing now."

"Emma, you've never been strong enough to take care of yourself," her mother said, her voice pleading. "You can see that, can't you? Oh, darling, come home. You belong here, with us."

Emma ignored the pleas and the claims. She'd been plenty strong—she should know. Her independence had been hard-won.

"He didn't abandon me, Daddy," she said. "He came to see me every day. He called when he was in Bahania for his aunt's funeral, and as soon as he got back to Texas, he practically camped out in front of the house, didn't he?"

"Is that what he told you?"

"Yes. Is he lying?"

Her father was silent for a long time. "He came by a few times."

She clutched the phone tighter. Reyhan had told the truth about everything. "You told him I didn't want to see him. You decided *for* me."

"Kitten, you were in no shape to deal with him. Have you forgotten what you went through?"

No. She would never forget. The pain would be with her always.

"Mom, did you write the letter telling him I never wanted to see him again?"

"I... Oh, Emma. It was for the best."

She closed her eyes and wondered how her life would have been different if she'd known. She'd loved Reyhan as much as her childish heart had allowed, and she would have gone with him in a second. Had her parents realized that? Had they not wanted to see their only child living half a world away in a foreign land?

If she had only known...

"What about the money?" she asked, more resigned than angry. "Why didn't you tell me about that?"

"We thought it was best for you not to worry about that," her mother said primly.

Not to worry? "I have student loans and a ten-year-old car," she said. "You had no right to keep that information to yourself. Spending it or giving it back was my decision to make."

"You were so young, kitten," her father said. "Too young."

For all of this, she thought.

"Reyhan said he sent a letter telling me not to let pride get in the way of the money. After that, some has been withdrawn regularly. What did you do with it?"

"We didn't spend it," her mother said, sounding outraged. "We simply moved it into a money-market account. It's all there, darling. I'll show you the bank statements when you get home."

She felt drained and weary. It had been an evening of too many emotions.

"Were you ever going to tell me the truth?" she asked.

"Of course," her mother said.

"We love you," her father added.

"When? Oh, let me guess. When you thought I was old enough."

"Exactly."

She was twenty-four and living on her own. She had a job, an apartment and something closely resembling a life. What rite of passage had her parents been waiting for?

She was sure in their hearts they had planned to tell her what had happened, but they would have put it off as long as possible. Partly because they wouldn't want to make her angry and partly because they wouldn't want her returning to Reyhan. She was beginning to suspect they would have done anything to keep her close. Even lie about her marriage.

"Why did you tell me the marriage wasn't real?" she asked.

"We weren't sure," her mother said. "That lawyer

we hired couldn't verify it one way or the other. Best to be safe.''

''By telling me I wasn't married when I was? What if I'd fallen in love and had gotten married again? I would have been a bigamist.''

''If you'd gotten serious about someone, we would have said something,'' her father told her. ''Emma, you have to understand our position in all this. We only want what's best for you.''

Words she'd heard her entire life. For a long time she'd believed them, but now she wasn't so sure. Did they want what was best for her or for themselves?

''I need to go,'' she said. ''I'll call when I get home.''

''Emma, no!'' Her mother sounded frantic. ''You can't stay there. It's so far away.''

''I'll be back in two weeks. Don't worry. Everything is fine.''

''But, Emma—''

She cut them off with a quick ''I love you'' then hung up.

Alone, confused and weary to her bones, she curled up in a corner of her sofa and wondered when exactly her life had become so messy and what she was going to do to get things in order.

Chapter Five

The next morning Emma awoke with a brain full of questions and an achy feeling low in her belly. She knew the latter came from a night of erotic dreams with her and Reyhan as the stars. In her sleep he'd taken her over and over again and she'd been a willing participant. She'd pleaded and wanted and touched and surrendered happily.

Uneasy and more than a little apprehensive, Emma decided to ignore whatever not-so-subconscious message might be lurking in her dreams. Right now she had bigger problems—namely, what she'd said to Reyhan and how he'd told the truth about everything.

After showering in her Montana-size bathroom and dressing, she skipped breakfast. She owed Reyhan an apology and the nerves clog dancing in her stomach were unlikely to go away until she'd delivered it.

After getting directions to his office from the young woman cleaning the suite, Emma stepped out into the main corridor and walked toward what she hoped was the business wing of the palace. Ten minutes and three more sets of directions later, she walked into what looked like a very busy, very upscale office facility. She crossed to the middle-aged man sitting at a reception desk.

"I would like to speak with Prince Reyhan," she said.

The man's neutral expression didn't change but she thought she caught him eyeing her inexpensive dress and dismissing her.

"Do you have an appointment?" he asked.

She shook her head.

He reached for the large phone console on his desk. "I will call his assistant and check his schedule. May I ask who you are?"

She'd been about to say "Emma Kennedy" but her pride had been bruised. It wasn't her fault that she couldn't afford nice clothes. Besides, she was clean and tidy and she'd taken extra time with her makeup, and did Reyhan think she was badly dressed, too?

She raised her chin slightly and looked the man in the eye.

"His wife."

The man raised his eyebrows, color fled his cheeks and his jaw dropped.

"Of course, Your Highness." He nodded differentially and quickly pushed several buttons on the phone. When he was connected, he announced her and then hung up.

"This way, Princess Emma," he said, rising, then bowing.

Emma felt kind of small and petty for claiming a relationship that barely existed, but it was too late to call back the words.

She was led into a large open area. There were alcoves leading to private offices. The man apologized for making her wait even a second, then scurried off. Emma entertained herself by studying a color-coded map on the wall. She saw the capital city of Bahania and the ocean. El Bahar was also outlined and there were small markers at random intervals.

She moved closer to get a better look, when she felt a tingling at the back of her neck. Turning, she saw Reyhan striding toward her.

If her heart had not been trapped in her chest, it would have taken flight. He was so tall, she thought foolishly. And handsome. A powerful man who ruled an empire. Emotions flashed in his dark eyes but they were gone before she could catalog any of them. Then Reyhan was standing in front of her, staring, and Emma couldn't think. She could only breathe in the scent of him and silently wish he would kiss her again.

"Emma," he said, his voice low and sensual.

That was all. No more than her name and she found herself swaying toward him.

"Reyhan."

"Now that we have established our respective

identities, perhaps you would like to tell me the reason for your presence in my offices.''

"What? Oh.'' She glanced around at the people working. They were trying not to pay attention while hanging on every word. "Could we please speak in private?''

"Of course.''

He took her arm and led the way into a massive office. A carved wooden desk dominated the center of the room. An exquisite Oriental rug outlined a conversation area, while bookcases lined one entire wall.

She saw another detailed map opposite the window and three different computer systems.

"What is that for?'' she asked, pointing at the map.

"It details the placement of the oil wells and pumping stations here and in El Bahar.''

"There are a lot of them.''

He smiled slightly. "Yes.''

She'd heard Bahania was a rich nation—now she could see why.

"Our oil production is my area of expertise,'' he said. "That is why I was in Texas getting my master's degree.''

She thought of all the oil in her own state. "I guess we're experts, too.''

"Yes.''

He led her to the sofa grouping and motioned for her to sit down. When she'd done so, he settled across from her and assumed a patient expression.

Funny how he looked so remote and distant, she thought. As if he hadn't kissed her the previous evening. As if he hadn't reacted with desire, breathing

hard and wanting her. Or had she imagined his reaction? Had he kissed her to show he still had power
over her, while not reacting himself?

She didn't have enough experience to be able to
tell which it had been—a disadvantage she didn't enjoy because there was no doubt in her mind that Reyhan had known exactly what was going on inside of
her body.

"What did you wish to speak to me about?" he
asked.

She twisted her fingers together on her lap and
shrugged. "I spoke with my parents last night."

She waited to see if he would say anything, but
when he didn't, she continued.

"You were right…about everything. The marriage,
the money, that you tried to get in touch with me."

She glanced at him. He looked neither surprised
nor annoyed.

"I'm sorry I doubted you," she whispered.

"Why would you not?" he said. "You have
known your parents your entire life. We had been
together only a few weeks. I disappeared after the
wedding without giving you any information. Your
parents would have been suspicious. No doubt they
thought the worst."

"They're good at that," she said, surprised he was
being so magnanimous. She would have expected a
little gloating on his part—he'd more than earned it.

"I should have questioned them," she said. "I
wanted to, but I was afraid."

"That I sought you?"

"That you didn't. That I'd been far too forgettable."

He looked at her. "You are many things, Emma, but not that. I, too, could have put more effort into getting in touch with you. I suspected some subterfuge on the part of your father, but I walked away. I assumed that in time you would learn what had occurred and get in contact with me."

There was more to it than that, she thought. Reyhan was a proud man. He wouldn't beg. Not for her. Probably not for any woman.

"I should have been more curious," she told him. "Instead I took the easy way out and I believed them."

She studied the strong lines of his face. Who was this man who had married her and then walked away? If only she hadn't been so young and inexperienced. If only they'd met more as equals. Six years ago she might have intrigued him initially, but in time he would have tired of her childish ways. And now?

She didn't have an answer to that, although she was more than willing to try the kissing again. Not that Reyhan seemed to be offering.

"So all this time after the fact, we make peace with the past," she said. "And in a few days the king will authorize a divorce."

"Yes."

Ouch. His agreement stung a little. Foolish, she told herself. She couldn't possibly have any interest in him. Better to get this all behind her and start over. She would find someone else—someone more like her—and settle down. Have kids. That was her destiny—not a handsome prince from a foreign land.

She stood, and he rose, as well.

There was so much so say, and yet nothing. What could have been would stay a mystery.

"I was wondering about palace tours," she said.

He frowned. "What do you mean?"

"I'm unlikely to get back to Bahania anytime soon. I would like to take advantage of my remaining time here to see something of the palace and the city."

"You may go anywhere you like in the palace."

She laughed. "Gee, thanks, but wandering around lost isn't my idea of a good time. I'm interested in hearing about the palace itself. Maybe some of the history. Is there a regular tour offered? I could join that."

"I will take you anywhere you would like to go."

"That's really nice of you, but unnecessary. I know you're busy."

Not that she would mind spending time with Reyhan. Being around him made her insides flutter—a new and thrilling experience. But he had responsibilities that didn't include her.

"Until the divorce, you are my wife. I will show you the palace and the city. We will begin today after lunch."

"That sounds like more of an order than a request."

He smiled. "You were the one to mention the tour. I am accommodating you."

Hmm, if he said so. Emma figured there was no point in arguing. Not only would Reyhan likely win, but having the argument would prove her to be a complete idiot. She wanted to spend time with him, which he was offering. A smart woman would smile and say yes.

"I look forward to it," she said brightly. "What time?"

"Two o'clock. Is that convenient?"

She laughed. "It's not like I have a full social calendar. I'll be ready."

He reached out and took her hand, then drew it toward his mouth. At the last second, he turned her fingers and pressed his lips against the inside of her wrist.

The hot, damp contact sent shivers zipping up her arm. Tension invaded her body and she would swear her knees were within seconds of buckling.

"Until two," he said, and released her.

Emma left quickly while she could because the alternative seemed to be throwing herself at him and begging him to never let her go. A feeling she couldn't deny, nor could she explain.

Reyhan showed up promptly at two. While he still looked hunky and appealing in the suit he'd been wearing earlier, Emma had agonized over her clothing choices. She'd wanted to look sexy and glamorous and enticing. All a challenge based on the contents of her suitcase. Not that her closet back home would have been that much help. She spent her workdays in scrub pants and brightly colored shirts and her evening attire pretty much consisted of khaki pants or long skirts and casual tops. Not exactly the fashion-forward clothing she would need to catch the eye of a prince.

A prince very interested in divorcing her, she reminded herself as she smoothed the front of her skirt and smiled brightly. Reyhan had made it more than clear he was intent on getting her out of his life. Not exactly the actions of a man prepared to be overwhelmed by her modest charms.

"What interests you most?" he asked as she stepped into the hallway and shut the door of her suite behind her. "There is an impressive display of centuries-old jewelry in a few of the public rooms."

"I'm sure it's lovely," she told him, "but I'm more of an antique furniture and tapestry kind of girl."

Reyhan raised one dark eyebrow, but didn't comment on her statement. Maybe he didn't believe her, which wasn't her problem. Sure, she liked sparkling things as much as the next woman, but they weren't her world.

"Very well," he said. "We'll begin in the older section of the palace. The original structure was built in the late 900s. Since then, the pink palace has been updated and enlarged several times. Once, during the reign of Elizabeth the first, the daughter of a wealthy merchant was captured and held for ransom by the bastard son of the king. After a time, instead of returning her, he fell in love with her. They married and lived happily together. For their tenth anniversary, he presented her with a chapel—a miniature representation of a cathedral she'd seen once in France. We'll begin there."

Emma walked next to him, trying not to get caught up in the heat his body generated. "Were many women captured and held against their will?"

Reyhan smiled. "It is a time-honored tradition for sheiks to take that which they admire."

How comforting. "So there's a harem here in the palace, too?"

"Of course."

She wasn't sure if she wanted to see it or not. Imagine a place where women were held simply to offer pleasure to one man. Of course there would be a lot of free time. She could catch up on her reading.

She glanced at her estranged husband and wondered what it would be like to be captured by him. Would he be kind? Demanding? She shivered at the thought of either. The wanting that was always just below the surface when he was around, burst into life. Her body ached to be close to his. She wanted him to pull her against him, kiss her, caress her. Instead she had to be content with the occasional brush of his arm against hers.

"Do men in Bahania have more than one wife?" she asked.

"No. That practice died out long before it was outlawed. Men quickly came to realize that keeping one wife happy was a full-time job."

"I've never understood why the multiple-wife thing was so popular," she said as they stepped out into a beautiful formal garden. She recognized it as the one she could see from her balcony. Where Cleo and her husband had come to be alone.

"It would be easy for a woman to be with more

than one man in an evening, but after men, um, have their way, they're sort of out of it for a while.''

Halfway through her sentence, she realized she'd stepped into some very dangerous territory. Did she *really* want to be having this conversation with Reyhan?

He stared at her, his expression unreadable but not the least bit friendly. ''You know this from personal experience?''

''No. I've just…heard.''

''It is not about pleasure,'' he told her, his voice slightly strained. ''It is about children. A woman is with child for nine months. In that time, a man can continue to impregnate other women, while she can only bear him one son at a time.''

''Oh. That makes sense.'' She spoke brightly, as if this conversation was no big deal. ''Good point. What's that?''

She pointed at a large statue of a horse rearing. It was life-size and pure white.

''A gift from the king of El Bahar some years ago. We have always had close ties with our neighbor.''

''I remember hearing that.''

Reyhan led the way down a narrow path. Lush plants grew on both sides and tall trees offered shade. It was early April and still pleasant but she was sure by mid-July the temperature, even in morning, would be unbearable.

''Here we are,'' he said, pointing to a small but exquisitely built chapel.

Spires reached toward the heavens. All of the windows were stained glass and looked ancient. Stone steps led into a darkened and cool interior.

Emma walked inside and instantly felt at peace. Half a dozen pews flanked a wide center aisle. In front, more stained-glass windows stretched up to the arched ceiling.

"Master craftsmen were brought in from France," Reyhan told her. "They worked for three years on the chapel, all in secret. While they were here, they trained many local masons who incorporated the designs in their own work."

Emma touched the carved wood pews. The finish was thick and glossy, obviously well cared for. What a private treasure, she thought.

"Are services ever held here?" she asked.

"On special holidays."

She fought a sudden longing to attend one, knowing she would be gone and forgotten before the next occasion.

Reyhan led her back into the palace. They walked down several flights of stone stairs, until she was sure they were underground.

"Long-lost treasures were recently returned to us," he said, pushing opening a massive wooden door. "Tapestries and statues, along with jewels and pieces of furniture. Local experts are restoring our history to us."

He showed her a wall-size tapestry in a frame. Two women matched threads and carefully repaired a large tear. It took Emma a second to see the scene—four men galloping across the desert. Their expressions were intent and fierce, their faces slightly familiar.

She glanced at Reyhan, noting the similarity in the shape of the eyes and build of the bodies.

"Relatives?" she asked.

"Ancestors. This dates back to the 1200s."

She wanted to touch the cloth, but knew too much handling could damage the delicate treasure.

He showed her shelves of statues and stacks of carved furniture. "Pieces are moved around in the palace," he said. "Some things are on display here in the city museum. Others are sent on tour around the world."

"I can't imagine what it would have been like growing up here," she said as they left the storage area and climbed stairs to the main level.

"As a young child, I had little use for the past. It was simply information I needed to learn to please my tutors."

"I suppose. We never appreciate what we have when we're young. Not unless we lose it."

He glanced at her. "What did you lose?"

She thought of her childhood. Loving, if overly protective. "I'm not sure there was anything. I was speaking in general." She glanced around at the city-size rooms they passed. "I think my entire house could have fit in there. You and your brothers must have had a good time playing hide-and-seek in here."

"We were not permitted to play games in the main rooms of the palace."

"Probably just as well. You could have gotten lost for days."

"Our tutors would have come looking for us."

Tutors. Not exactly a reference she could relate to. "You didn't go to the local schools?"

"No. When I was eleven I was sent to boarding school in Britain."

"It's that whole prince thing, huh?"

He glanced at her. One corner of his mouth curved up. "Prince thing?"

She grinned. "You know. Being royal. It made you different."

"We were given many unique opportunities."

"I suppose you would have to learn things regular kids didn't. Like how to behave in certain situations, and rules about running a country. Of course I'll bet each of you had your own horse. I guess it's a trade-off. There are advantages and disadvantages to most circumstances."

They walked into a huge reception room. The ceilings had to be three stories tall. There were carved poles and an intricately inlaid marble floor. Floor-to-ceiling beveled windows let in light. A raised stage stood at one end of the incredible room.

"My apartment doesn't even have a foyer," she murmured, and wondered again why he'd bothered with her all those years ago. "I was little more than a country mouse."

"What?"

She motioned to the gold light fixtures. "I'm going to guess that color isn't just a really nice paint job. Those are real gold."

"Yes, but it is of little consequence."

"Perhaps to you." She turned in a slow circle. Reyhan's leaving her was for the best, she thought sadly. There was no way she could have fit in here then. No way she fit in now.

"Is there another man?" he asked abruptly.

She stared at him. "What? You mean am I seeing anyone?"

He nodded.

"No. I'm not dating anyone right now. I've never been very good at the whole boy-girl thing, but you would know that better than anyone."

Memories crept in of their three nights together after their wedding. How he had taken her over and over and how she'd been unable to be anything but afraid.

Things would be different now, she thought with regret. She was sure she could respond, even hunger for him. But a man intent on getting a divorce was unlikely to be physically interested in the woman he was leaving behind—passionate kisses aside.

"Once you are no longer married, you can change that," he said.

"As can you."

But she didn't want to think about him being with another woman.

"It's scary to think what could have happened," she said to distract herself. "I really didn't know about the marriage being real. If I'd gotten serious about someone and we'd wanted to get married…" Would her parents have told her the truth? She would like to think so, but she was no longer sure about anything.

"I would have been in touch to let you know we were still married."

"How would you have known?"

He stared at her without speaking, and then realization sank in. "You've kept track of me." It was a statement, not a question. She wasn't sure if she was pleased or creeped out.

"At first, I received monthly reports," he told her. "Now, yearly. You are my wife. It is my duty to watch over you."

As he hadn't known about her job, the last report must have been sometime last summer, after her graduation but before she'd started work at the hospital.

"If I'd known we were still married, I would have contacted you," she said. "I mean, being married all these years and being apart doesn't make any sense." She realized how that sounded. "Not that I'm suggesting we *should* have been together."

"I understand. Divorcing is the most sensible plan."

"Right."

Sure. It wasn't as if she knew anything about Reyhan, save the fact that being within ten feet of him reduced her to a quivering mass.

"I wonder what would have happened if I'd known you'd come back for me," she said. "Would you have brought me here?"

"Of course. As my wife, your place is at my side."

"What about my education? I wouldn't have been able to go to college here."

"Should we argue about what never was?"

"Probably not."

But everything would have been different. They would have had children by now. She'd always wanted children, she thought wistfully. And with Reyhan as their father, they would be stronger than her. More able to stand up for themselves.

Would she have been able to keep him happy? Would their marriage have flourished or would her youth have worn on his affections?

Had he loved her, even a little? More questions she wouldn't be asking.

"Reyhan…"

She spoke his name, then paused, not sure what she wanted to say or ask.

He stared at her, his dark eyes narrowing slightly.

"Stop," he ordered.

"What?"

Her chest tightened as it became difficult to breathe. Awareness flickered through her body, making her tremble. Her mouth went dry, her fingers tingled and wanting swelled until she thought she would burst.

Then she was in his arms with no way to understand how she'd come to be there. He held her tightly, possessively and she reveled in belonging to him even for that single moment.

She had less than a heartbeat to anticipate the kiss before he pressed his mouth against hers and claimed her.

She parted instantly, wanting the intimacy, needing to make him desire her. The melting began, in her chest and between her thighs. At the first brush of his tongue against hers, she closed her eyes. At the second, she held in a sigh of contentment. Passion flooded every part of her body, making her squirm to get closer.

She touched his shoulders, his arms, then ran her hands up and down his muscled back. His fingers tangled in her hair. Their tongues stroked and circled and danced before he pulled back slightly and kissed her jaw.

He nibbled his way to her ear where he drew the lobe into his mouth and sucked gently. Her breath caught. He dropped his hands to her hips, then to her fanny where he cupped her curves before pulling her hard against him. As her stomach nestled against him, she felt a bulge.

Fierce gladness flashed through her. Reyhan was aroused. She excited him as much as he excited her. The thought thrilled her then was lost as he licked the sensitive skin under her ear, and she was unable to think about anything other than the exquisite sensations he created.

Heat was everywhere. His fingers burned, his body warmed. She found herself wanting to strip off clothing and bare herself. The large room and hard marble floors offered neither privacy nor comfort, but she didn't care.

She breathed his name, and when his mouth returned to hers, she was the one to slip her tongue against his lower lip before dipping inside.

He tasted faintly of coffee, with a little sweetness she couldn't explain. He continued to press against her, rubbing his arousal against her belly. She wanted to raise herself up on tiptoe so he could rub her *there* and pleasure them both.

One of his hands moved from her rear to her hip, then traveled higher. Her breasts swelled in anticipation of his touch. She wrapped both arms around his neck and clung to him so that when he reached his destination, she would not collapse at his feet.

Closer and closer and closer until she nearly begged him out loud. At last he cupped her right breast and brushed his thumb against her tight nipple.

Pleasure jolted her like lightning. She gasped, then nipped at his lower lip while he continued to stroke her. She could feel tension building between her thighs, the dampness of her panties and the trembling in her legs.

And then he was gone. He stepped back and stared at her. His breath came in rapid pants. Passion brightened his eyes and tightened the lines of his face. She didn't have the courage to glance lower, to *see* that he wanted her, but she knew.

They stared at each other for what seemed like an eternity. Emma wished she knew what to say, or even how to ask why he'd stopped when they were both so obviously willing. But nothing in her life had prepared her for such a reaction, so she couldn't find the words.

"I must return to my office," Reyhan said at last. "You will find your way back to your rooms."

It was a statement rather than a question, and Emma wasn't sure she could speak, let alone argue. She watched him walk away, then she staggered a few feet to one of the columns and leaned against it until her heartbeat slowed to normal.

She didn't understand what was happening with

Reyhan. She hadn't seen him in years. Why was he getting to her? And why did he have to be the only man who made her *want* with such incredible intensity?

"Too many questions," she whispered when she could finally think and breathe like a normal person. "No answers." Just a man who made her burn and a ticking clock that reminded her it would soon be time to leave.

Reyhan didn't return to his office right away. He detoured through the far end of the palace, walking briskly in an attempt to burn off the passion and need that Emma had created.

Nothing had changed. Emma's pull over him remained absolute. She could bring him to his knees with just a glance. When she touched him—he would capture the moon if she so requested.

He could never let her know the power she had over him, could never let her know his weakness for her. He paused by a window and stared uneasily out at the view. He *would* control this, he told himself. He would *stay* in control.

In a few days she would be gone and there would be relief. But instead of anticipation, he felt only pain at the thought of his world without her. The ache inside of him deepened.

So much time had passed, he'd hoped that he could face her and not care, not need. But he'd been wrong. Worse, she responded to him with the wants and desires of an experienced woman. She was no longer the frightened child he'd married.

Who had taught her to kiss so expertly? he wondered grimly. What man had tutored the woman who belonged to *him?* Passion blended with rage as his hands curled into fists. Were that man here now, Reyhan would rip him apart.

No! Control. He had to get control. Emma might be the color in his world, but she was also dangerous. Better to live in shades of gray than risk everything. Just a few more days. Then she would be gone and he would be free.

Chapter Six

The main marketplace was so filled with light and color, it was like stepping inside of a kaleidoscope. Emma didn't know where to look first. Wooden stalls lined the wide stone street and everywhere she turned there were more wonders to be seen. Bright silks puddling like quivering gems, copper pots of every shape and size, fruits, vegetables and rich, supple leather goods tempted her to step closer and touch.

In addition to the visual display, there were also strange and intriguing scents—sandalwood, coconut, exotic flowers and spices blended with wood smoke and the underlying musk of perfumes. A hundred conversations blended into a unique musical accompaniment with the call of the merchants, the barking of dogs and the laughter of the children racing through the back alleys.

"It's wonderful," she breathed, pausing to stare into the eyes of a camel tied up at a corner. "Like something out of a movie."

She smiled at Reyhan, who nodded.

"There are few sights that compare with an open-air market," he told her. "We have one of the oldest and largest in the world."

She smiled at a young woman holding a baby. The woman ducked her head and slowly backed away. Emma knew it wasn't because of her—no one knew her from a rock. Instead it was the presence of a prince, and the three large and hostile-looking bodyguards that were assigned to accompany them. The well-dressed and well-armed men kept the other shoppers at least an arm's distance away and discouraged casual conversation.

Emma wanted to protest, saying they would be fine on their own, but who was she to judge? Besides, Reyhan had explained that the accompanying men were as much for crowd control as protection.

She'd been surprised when Reyhan had offered to take her to the local market. After their last encounter she'd been sure he would want to avoid her, what with how he'd stalked away without saying anything. Yet two days later he'd shown up at her door with the invitation.

She'd been delighted to accept.

"Local dates," Reyhan said, stopping by one of the stands. "Try some."

The merchant, a tiny wizened man with a huge

smile, held out a tray of plump dates. When he nodded encouragingly at her, she took one and tasted.

"They're good," she said.

The merchant beamed. Reyhan reached into his
pocket and pulled out a few coins.

"No, no." The old man backed up and shook his
head. "It is my honor. My pleasure."

Reyhan smiled. "Such is the power of a beautiful
woman."

Emma was so startled by the offhand compliment,
she laughed. "Oh, sure. He's overwhelmed by my
beauty, not by the fact that you're a prince and traveling with enough muscle to start your own wrestling
federation."

His dark gaze settled on her face. "You don't think
you're attractive?"

"I'm okay." Passably pretty, she thought. No one
had ever looked at her and then run shrieking in the
opposite direction. "But I've never overwhelmed
anyone."

He continued to study her, then looked away without saying anything. The merchant pressed a bag in
her hands. She could feel the soft fruit inside.

"Thank you," she said. "You're very kind."

As they walked away, Reyhan said something in a
language she couldn't understand. One of the bodyguards made a note on a small pad he'd pulled from
his jacket pocket.

"What was that about?" she asked when they'd
drifted down another aisle in the market.

"Someone from the palace will visit the old man's
stall later in the week," Reyhan said in a low voice.

"A large quantity of dates will be purchased at a premium price." He jerked his head back the way they'd come. "The old man offered a gift he can scarcely afford to give. Respect from my people shouldn't come at the price of starving."

"It was just a few dates."

"He has nothing else to sell."

An interesting point, she thought, studying Reyhan from the corner of her eye. She would have said he was firm and intelligent. Remote and stern with a hidden well of passion. But she would never have guessed he had a compassionate heart for those in need. One more item on the long list of things she didn't know about her soon-to-be ex prince-husband.

Two young boys ran past them, laughing and yelling as they went. Emma turned to watch them go.

"Did you come play in the market when you were a child?" she asked. "Were you allowed out and about?"

"Sometimes," Reyhan said. "With my brother Jefri." He shrugged. "Once we were playing with more abandon than usual and knocked a cooking pot off an open fire. In our hasty effort to retrieve it before the large and mean-looking owner noticed, we bumped a burning log into the corner of a stall. It was old, dry wood and went up in seconds."

She covered her mouth with her fingers. "Was anyone hurt?"

He shook his head. "No, but three stalls were completely destroyed before the fire was brought under control. Jefri and I were in trouble for a long time. Our father refused to let us simply pay for the damage out of our pocket money. Instead we had to rebuild the stalls and then work in them for several weekends. In the end, the owners came out ahead as people shopped to see the young princes up close.''

''So it was a fitting punishment?'' she asked, even as she thought it sounded a bit harsh. Not the rebuilding. That made sense, but the working in public where the boys would be stared at like zoo animals.

''My father wanted us to learn,'' Reyhan told her, not really answering the question. ''Jefri and I were more careful on our next trip to the marketplace.''

They stopped in front of a stall displaying silver jewelry. The merchant nodded exuberantly and held out dozens of silver bangles. They were large and beautifully carved.

''Something to remember the day by,'' Reyhan said, selecting several and offering them to her.

She wouldn't need a reminder. Everything about this time with him was burned onto her brain. But the bracelets *were* pretty. She reached for one made of linked hearts and slid it on.

He took the bag of dates from her and passed them to one of the bodyguards, then held her hand out in front of her. When he turned her wrist, the light caught the shiny bangle.

''Very nice,'' he said, and gave the jeweler several folded bills.

''Is it terribly expensive?'' she asked, feeling a little guilty. ''I can pay you back. I have my checkbook in my purse.''

Reyhan didn't speak, nor did he turn away. His dark gaze did the talking for him as she remembered who he was and all the money he'd left in her account. No doubt a silver bracelet wasn't going to be a blip on his financial radar.

"Thank you," she said softly. "It's very beautiful."

"You are a woman who deserves beautiful things."

That compliment nearly made her stumble, but she managed to stay upright. Fake it until you believe it, she told herself. Even if the faking lasted right up until the moment she walked into her apartment back in Dallas.

She wanted to ask what made her deserving of beautiful things and if he meant it when he looked at her with fire in his eyes. Did he feel the sparks between them? Did the heat draw him? Had he relived their kisses, as she had, longing for more, for every intimacy?

Rather than risk a potentially embarrassing line of conversation, she went for something safer.

"Did you attend school locally?" she asked.

"No. Just the tutor, then to a British prep school, then an American university."

He placed his hand on the small of her back and urged her down another crowded aisle. Several people bowed and smiled when they saw him. From what she could tell, Reyhan was very popular with his people. Probably a good thing when one was a prince.

"My father thought it was important for his sons to have a diverse education and contact with the West. Much of our business is conducted with American and European interests. Familiarity with mindsets and customs helps the process.''

She thought of her own small life. Aside from now, and except for their brief honeymoon in the Caribbean, she'd never been out of the state.

''I would imagine both Britain and America were different for you,'' she said.

''I knew some of your ways from watching movies. I'd been raised speaking English as well as Bahanian, so I was comfortable with the language. But there were still lessons to be learned.''

She stopped and touched his arm. ''Like what?''

He glanced at her. ''When I first arrived at my university, I told a few people who I was. Word quickly spread and my time there became…difficult.''

''Everyone wanting to rub shoulders with a real, live prince?'' she asked sympathetically.

''Something like that. Some young women were enthusiastic in their effort to get to know me.''

She could imagine. ''You would have been something of a catch.''

One corner of his mouth curved up. ''So I was told. When I went to Texas, I decided not to tell anyone who I was. A few recognized me from various articles in magazines and reports on television, but for the most part I was able to simply be myself.''

''I had no clue,'' she said, more than a little embarrassed by the fact. ''I guess I should have paid more attention to current events.''

He started walking again and drew her along with him. ''Not at all. Your interest in me was about who I was as a person, not who I was as a prince.''

"The whole royalty thing would have overwhelmed me," she admitted. "Actually, I would have run in the opposite direction."

"And I would have chased after you."

"Really?"

She glanced at him, wondering if he was teasing or telling the truth. Would Reyhan have pursued her? She wanted to believe he had been that interested, but was it really possible? She'd just been a very shy, inexperienced eighteen-year-old. Hardly the sort of woman to catch the interest of a sophisticated man of the world.

He took her hand in his and squeezed lightly. "You wanted to be a nurse. I know you graduated with honors, but I'm not that familiar with your work. Tell me what you do."

It was difficult to concentrate with his fingers rubbing against hers. When his thumb brushed against her palm, she nearly moaned. Wanting burned low in her belly, making her ache and need.

So many physical reactions, she thought. Why was her body coming alive now? With him?

Better not to ask, she told herself and focused on Reyhan's question.

"I'm a delivery room nurse," she said.

His expression tightened with surprise. "You assist with births?"

"Pretty much." She smiled. "It's so wonderful to spend my day helping babies being born. It's a time of joy and happiness for everyone involved."

"I suppose that is more fitting than you dealing with men."

"That's not why I chose my specialty. I went into it because I love children and babies and I thought it would be very gratifying. I was right."

"My sister-in-law recently had a baby. My sisters Zara and Sabrina are also pregnant."

"I'd heard. Cleo told me."

As she spoke, she raised her face toward his. Sunlight turned strands of her hair to the color of copper. Humor brightened her eyes and made her skin glow as if lit from within.

Beautiful, Reyhan thought desperately. She had always been beautiful.

Not that her being ugly would have helped, for if he closed his eyes when he was with her, he still wanted her. The sound of her voice was as musical as the rush of the tide. The scent of her body teased and enticed him. Her gentle spirit called to him, as did her intelligence and humor. Blind, deaf and mute, he would have burned for the lightest brush of her touch.

His need for her grew every second he was in her presence. Soon it would be as uncontrollable as a wild animal, and like that animal, he was in danger of devouring her. He had to get away from her but not just yet. One more day, he told himself. Then he would retreat to nurse his wounds and wait out her remaining time in his company.

"What will you do when you return to Dallas?" he asked.

"What do you mean? I'll go back to work."

Amusement tempered his growing desire. "Because you have bills to pay?"

She laughed. "Yes. All the usual things like rent and utilities, plus my student loans."

She was still so innocent.

"I am Prince Reyhan of Bahania."

She blinked at him. "Actually, I know that."

"You are my wife."

She shook her head. "I suppose technically, although not really."

"Legally you are."

"Okay. I guess. But you want a divorce."

"And after the divorce, do you think you'll leave with nothing?"

Emma's green eyes widened in surprised. "I don't want anything. I'm not your responsibility, and I'm perfectly capable of taking care of myself."

How like her, he thought. Other women of his acquaintance would be trying to squeeze out every dollar they could.

"I will provide for you," he told her. "Arrangements will be made for you to purchase a house, then I will set up a checking account as I did before."

"You really don't have to do this."

"I know."

"But we were only together for a few days."

It should have been for a lifetime.

The thought came unbidden. Reyhan did his best to chase it away, but it stayed in place. Stubborn, real and tempting. So much would have been different if he'd simply insisted on her returning with him. When his aunt had died, he'd left Emma behind, to spare her the trauma of finding out who and what he was. He didn't want to thrust her into royal life without some time to get used to the idea, nor did he want her meeting his family at a funeral. But by leaving her behind, he'd lost her.

How would their lives have been different if he'd brought her home right away? She would be a mother by now. His wife in every sense of the word. How would she have handled the responsibilities, the traditions? Would she have grown into them or chafed at the restrictions?

He would never know—about any of it. She could not be his wife; he had chosen a different path. But perhaps they could pretend for a single day.

"All the women I've ever met love to shop," he said. "Are you different in that, as well?"

She smiled. "I don't mind spending an afternoon or two at the mall. Are you trying to tempt me into accepting your more-than-generous offer of a settlement?"

"Not at all. The money will be provided. You don't have a choice in the matter."

She shook her head. "You're pretty high-handed."

"Yes."

She laughed. "That's it. Just a yes? Aren't you going to protest?"

"I get what I want one way or another."

"Must be nice."

"It is."

Except when he wouldn't allow himself what he wanted.

"This way," he said, taking her arm and leading her through the marketplace. The bodyguards trailed along behind.

Emma knew there was no point in protesting or asking where they were going. Reyhan would tell her when he was ready. Besides, she was enjoying her time with him to the point that it didn't much matter to her what came next.

She glanced down at the bangle on her wrist. Something to remember him by, she thought fondly. Not gold and expensive jewels, which weren't her style. Just a simple, silver bracelet.

They turned a corner onto a main street, then stopped in front of a plain storefront. She glanced at the sign that read Aimee's before Reyhan moved inside.

The cool interior was a contrast to the warmth of the afternoon. Emma took in the cream-on-white decorations, the elegant displays of clothing and shoes and instantly felt frumpy in her outlet-sale clothing.

A tall, painfully thin woman approached. "Yes, may I—" The woman touched her perfectly coiffed hair, then smiled. "Prince Reyhan. A pleasure. How may I serve you?"

"This is Emma," he said. "My wife."

The woman's dark eyes widened as she nodded graciously. "Princess. I am Aimee. Welcome to my shop."

Emma offered a smile even as she wondered what Reyhan was doing. It was one thing to tell people they were married in the palace, but why would he do it in public? No one had known they were married and they were going to be divorced very soon. Why bother with the hassle of explaining?

"She needs a complete wardrobe," he continued.

Emma turned to him. "What?"

"Indulge me."

"But..." Aware of the older woman's obvious interest in what was going on, Emma lowered her voice and leaned in close. "I don't need a new wardrobe. Mine is fine. I'm not saying her clothes aren't lovely, but they've got to be really pricey and they don't fit into my regular world."

"You're not in your regular world now, Emma. You're in mine. You're also a beautiful woman who deserves beautiful things. It pleases me to buy these for you."

Protesting too much seemed both ungracious and stupid. Instead she nodded. "Thank you for your kindness."

How bad could it be? she thought as she followed the well-dressed store owner into the dressing room area. A couple of dresses, maybe a pair of jeans or two and she would be done. Reyhan didn't strike her as the kind of man who would enjoy waiting while a woman tried on clothing.

Or was he?

Two hours later Emma was less sure about everything. Reyhan had been remarkably patient as she'd been dressed in everything from simple sundresses to suits to elegant evening wear. Whenever something looked especially nice on her, Aimee urged her to step out into the main salon for him to see. Much to her chagrin, he'd been the one to make the decisions on what to buy and what not to.

"These are supposed to be *my* clothes," she said

as he shook his head over a dark pants suit she quite liked.

"Too severe," he told her. "The cut is too loose."

"I can't spend my day flashing cleavage at the world."

"No. That you save for me."

Instinctively she pressed a hand against the vee neck of the suit. Was he talking as the powerful husband and prince or as man? Were they different? She stared at him, trying to figure out what he was thinking and what he wanted from her. The strong, handsome lines of his face gave away nothing.

But his words had made her *aware* of him again. While she'd been busy trying on outfit after outfit she'd been able to forget the tension lurking just under the surface. She'd managed to forget how much she liked being close to him and how he'd made her feel when he'd kissed her. Now she remembered everything.

"This will be fabulous," Aimee said when Emma returned to the dressing room. The older woman held out a strapless beaded gown in bronze. "The color will bring out the fire in your hair. Perhaps the prince will buy you a necklace of yellow diamonds to complete the look."

Yeah, right. Like that was going to happen. Emma didn't think that soon-to-be divorced wives rated rare gemstones. Of course she hadn't thought they rated new wardrobes, either.

After stripping off the pants suit, she studied the dress. No way was she going to be able to keep on her bra. Aimee stepped outside to give her privacy, so Emma continued undressing until she stood in just her panties, then she stepped into the elegant gown.

It fit her perfectly, sliding over her hips as if it had been made for her. Aimee returned with a pair of strappy sandals and some combs to hold back Emma's hair.

"Excellent," the woman said approvingly. "You look exactly like the princess you are."

Emma glanced in the mirror, then did a double take. She *did* look royal, or at least elegant in a way she never had before.

"I guess clothes really do make the woman," she murmured as she walked out into the salon.

Reyhan looked up from a newspaper, then rose to his feet and nodded. "Yes. That is exactly right. You are stunning."

"Thank you. The dress is amazing and I know it fits great, but there's no way I'm going to keep it."

"Why not?"

"Reyhan, where will I ever wear it? I really appreciate your interest in my wardrobe, but be serious. This isn't me."

He dropped the paper onto the small table by his chair and walked toward her. When he was less than a foot away, he stopped and looked into her face.

She met his gaze and felt the impact of his intense stare. Heat grew until she felt uncomfortable in the strapless gown. She wanted to tug down the hidden zipper and let the dress pool at her feet. She wanted to be naked before him. Naked and vulnerable and slick with wanting. Need made her ache deep inside. Her thighs trembled.

"It pleases me to buy you these things," he said, his voice hoarse. "Why do you object?"

Why, indeed. At this moment, she could deny him nothing. If only he would say that he wanted her. If only he would touch her. Anywhere. Her arms, her face, her breasts. She felt her tight nipples rub against the soft lining of the gown and wished the contact to be against Reyhan's palms instead.

Take me.

She didn't speak the words, but somehow he heard. Fire erupted in his eyes. His muscles tensed and his breathing quickened.

When his gaze shifted to the entrance to the dressing room, she knew what he was thinking. That they could be alone there. Right now. No waiting, no wondering if it was right. Just a man and woman taking pleasure in each other.

It was insane to even consider such a thing, but she wanted to. Desperately. They could—

The click of heels on the tile floor cut through the erotic silence. Before Emma could object, Aimee came out of the back room and Reyhan turned away. It was as if the moment had never been. Reluctantly she returned to the dressing room and took off the dress.

Later, when their limo was filled with boxes and bags from the boutique, and Reyhan sat so carefully at the opposite end of the long leather seat, she tried to figure out what was going on between them.

Six years ago, after their brief marriage ceremony, they'd retired to a hotel suite and spent three days together. Emma remembered the intimacy of making love with him. There had been little desire on her part. Mostly she'd felt embarrassment, fear and occasionally pain. The more Reyhan had wanted her, the more scared she'd become. When he'd been called back to Bahania, she'd been grateful.

Back then she'd simply endured his desires, whereas now she shared them. What was different? Her? Had she grown up to the place where she could meet Reyhan as an equal? Had he changed? Was it chemistry or timing? Was it a quirk of fate that she would find herself falling for a man who planned on divorcing her then have her disappear from his life forever?

Emma paced the length of her suite. She'd already unpacked her beautiful clothes and admired them while trying not to look at the price tags. Some of her evening gowns cost as much as a good used car. She had no idea where she would wear them, but that was really the least of her problems. Instead there was the pressing matter of Reyhan.

What was going on between them? Was acting on their mutual attraction a good thing or would it make her a nominee for idiot of the year? Should she say something to him? Ask him if he'd changed his mind about the divorce? Ask him if he just wanted her for sex? Ignore the whole thing and count the hours until she headed back for Dallas?

"If you were the least bit brave, you'd talk to him," she murmured to herself. "Put it all out on the table and see what happens."

A sensible plan.

She crossed to the phone, intent on calling him at his office, but before she could there was a knock on her suite door.

Reyhan? Her heart pounded at the thought. She replaced the phone and hurried to the door.

But instead of her handsome husband, a young maid stood in the hallway. The girl handed her a note, nodded and left. Emma closed the door, then unfolded the piece of paper. As she read, her chest tightened and her spirits sank.

Emma,
My thanks for a lovely day. Unfortunately, some minor trouble in the oil fields calls me away. By the time you read this I will have left by helicopter. I'm not sure of the date of my return, but I will make sure it is before you leave Bahania for good.

Disappointment swelled inside of her. He was gone and she might not see him again until it was time for her to go back to Dallas. Not exactly the actions of a man overwhelmed by passion. Had she misread him completely?

She hadn't been very good at understanding Reyhan when they'd first met. Apparently time and distance hadn't changed that fact.

"It's for the best," she whispered, crushing the note in her hands. "I'll go home and this will all be forgotten. I'll get on with my life. Find someone else and get married."

Although she had no idea who that someone else might be. Reyhan was going to be a tough act to follow.

Chapter Seven

"For a woman with a brand-new wardrobe, you're pretty down in the mouth," Cleo said the next morning.

Emma nuzzled baby Calah's sweet-smelling head and sighed. "It's guilt. Reyhan spent too much on me. The clothes are beautiful, but..."

Cleo rolled her eyes. "What? You don't deserve them? Emma, we're talking about the royal family. They've been rich for about a thousand years. Trust me. Your shopping spree didn't even count as pocket change."

Emma wanted to mention that the trip to the boutique hadn't been her idea, but she thought it might sound like she was making too big a deal of things. Cleo didn't think anything was out of the ordinary.

Reyhan hadn't minded. He'd wanted her to buy more than she had. The guilt was hers and she should deal with it by herself. Except...

"I didn't really need them."

Cleo laughed. "That's your mother talking. It's a very parental thing to say. Isn't it fun to buy things you *don't* need and not have to worry about cost? Think of this as the fulfillment of your every-female shopping fantasy. Besides, I know you made Reyhan happy. From what I can tell, all the princes like to take care of women. It can be occasionally annoying but for the most part it's pretty nice."

"So you're saying I went shopping just to keep *him* happy?"

"If it helps with the guilt, sure."

Emma smiled. "I'm going to look pretty silly wearing a beaded gown in the grocery store on Saturday morning."

"Not if you're over in the imported foods section. Tell everyone you're European."

"That might work." Emma thought of the beautiful evening gowns sitting in the suite's large closet. "Are there a lot of formal functions here at the palace?"

"Two or three each month. I've only just started attending them, what with being pregnant and all." She rubbed her baby's arm. "But now that Calah is here and I've had a chance to recover, I have social obligations, not to mention charitable ones."

"What do you mean?"

Cleo blew her daughter a kiss, then turned back to Emma. "I'm in a unique position to help people. In a way, that's a bigger dream fulfillment than the shopping. I've spoken with Sadik and the king, and I'm getting involved with homeless children. There aren't very many in Bahania and El Bahar, but it's a big problem in other countries. I had something of a twisted upbringing for my first few years and I know what it's like to be alone and scared. Sabrina and Zara, the king's other daughters, each have their causes. Sabrina's seriously into finding antiquities and returning them to their rightful countries so people can enjoy their heritage. Zara is a former professor. She's working on a network of scholarships for girls who want to go to college but can't afford it.''

"Sounds exciting," Emma said, hoping she didn't sound as wistful as she felt. Cleo was right. The chance to help people by using nearly unlimited resources would be a wonderful way to spend her life.

What would she have done if she and Reyhan had stayed together? She'd always loved children, especially babies. Maybe something with prenatal care. Not that she was going to get the chance to find out.

"How much longer do you have here?" Cleo asked. "I was hoping we could fit in a field trip so you could meet Sabrina and Zara. They live in a very interesting place."

"Not here in the city?"

"Not exactly."

When Cleo didn't seem willing to say anything else, Emma considered her question. "I was told I would be here two weeks, but I don't have an exact date for my return. I guess that's up to the king."

Not that she was all that anxious to head out, she

thought. Spending time with Reyhan had been exciting and fun and something she wouldn't mind doing more. But with him gone… She sighed. Her simple life had sure had gotten confusing.

"How are things with you and Reyhan?" Cleo asked. "Or is that too personal? I just meant it's been a long time. Is he the same guy you remembered?"

Emma chuckled. "Are we allowed to refer to a Bahanian prince as a guy?"

"Hmm, good point. We might be risking a beheading. Fortunately Calah is too young to turn us in."

Emma bounced the baby on her lap. "She would never betray us, would you, honey? You're one of the girls. We have to stick together." She looked at Cleo. "As for Reyhan being the same or different… Honestly, *everything* is different. When we met, I was a freshman, away from home for the first time in my life. He was a sophisticated older man who swept me off my feet. I spent most of our time together trying not to sound too young or stupid. That took most of my energy. I can't say I *did* ever know him."

"And now?"

Interesting question. "He's terrific. Not just those handsome dark good looks, either."

Cleo sighed. "Agreed. Sadik would be a catch even if he were a brainless fool. I could happily suspend my life simply looking at him. But there's a genuine person buried inside. I'm guessing Reyhan is the same."

"Yeah. He's smart and serious, but funny, too." And sexy. Too sexy, she thought remembering their almost close encounter in the boutique. She would have sworn he'd wanted her as much as she'd wanted him. So why had he just up and disappeared without seeing her to say goodbye?

"So the girl in you was overwhelmed the first time around," Cleo said. "How does the woman feel the second time around?"

"She's impressed," Emma admitted.

"Which doesn't make you sound like a woman who's hot for a divorce."

"Of course I am. Maybe not eager, but it's why I'm here. Reyhan is ready to get on with his life and his plan doesn't include me."

Cleo's blue eyes widened slightly. "You don't have to blindly agree, you know. You could take some time, see where things go."

Emma blinked at her. Could she? Was that an option? "I never thought I had a say in things."

"Arrogant princes prefer the world to do their bidding, but it doesn't always have to happen that way. You're half of the couple. You get a vote." She touched Emma's hand. "Seriously. If you're not sure what you want, tell the king. I'm sure he'd be more than willing to hold off the divorce for a while."

Tempting, Emma thought a half second before she shook her head. "No. There's no point. I don't belong here."

Cleo arched her eyebrows. "Oh, and I did? When I met Sadik I was the night manager of a copy shop. Not exactly princess material." She waved her fingers at the room. "It's not about the trappings, or even tradition. The king wants his sons to fall in love.

Prince Jefri has decided on an arranged match, but he's the only one.''

Cleo was wrong, Emma thought sadly. Reyhan wanted one, as well. He'd told her.

"Maybe if things had worked out differently when we'd first met," Emma said firmly. "But that time is past. We're different people. I have my own life back in Texas."

"Sure," Cleo said. "If you're not falling for Reyhan, there's no reason to stay. So tell me about your work in the hospital. You work in the delivery room, right?"

"Yes, it's wonderful."

Emma talked about a typical day, if there was such a thing, and how she loved what she did. But in the back of her mind, she kept hearing Cleo's words over and over again. *If you're not falling for Reyhan.*

She wasn't, she told herself firmly. She hadn't and she wouldn't. Falling for him after all these years apart would be just plain stupid. The fact that she enjoyed spending time with him was interesting but not significant. She wouldn't let it matter. She couldn't. Because Reyhan had made it clear he was only interested in moving on.

"They're making threats again," Will O'Rourke said quietly.

"The usual?" Reyhan asked from his place by the fire.

"Death and destruction. Interruption of oil production. The usual."

Reyhan kicked at a small rock in front of his chair.

"I would have more respect for these boys if they had a genuine complaint. We have neither taken their lands, nor displaced them."

"They want something for nothing. A share of the oil money or they make trouble. They're kids—seventeen or eighteen. To them this is a game."

"Extortion is a time-honored tradition all over the world." Reyhan turned his attention to the sky. It took a few seconds for his eyes to adjust to the total darkness, then he saw the thousands of stars twinkling in the heavens.

Beautiful, he thought. Mysterious. Distant. A world unto themselves. Much like Emma.

He shook his head. The point of his trip to the desert had been to avoid her, but if he was going to spend all his time thinking about her, then he might as well torture himself by being in her presence.

"I doubt they have a plan," Will said.

It took Reyhan a moment to remember what they'd been talking about. The teenage renegades.

"They imagine themselves to be characters in a movie," he told his security chief. "They will ride their purebred Bahanian stallions to victory."

Reyhan had no more patience for these boys. He'd listened to their grievances and investigated their claims. They had not been pushed off their lands, nor injured in any way by the oil production. Most of them were bored second sons from hardworking nomadic families. Unable to inherit, they didn't want to work to acquire their wealth. Instead they sought to take that which belonged to the people.

"Watch them," Reyhan said. "In time they will grow bored and go home."

"You hired me to keep the peace, then made it impossible for me to do my job."

"To date there have been threats, but no actions. They are afraid of you. I consider that doing your job."

Will was a former army ranger who had grown up on oil rigs in the Gulf of Mexico. His unique combination of knowledge and skills had made him a find. Over the past three years he'd worked his way up from the person in charge of security to Reyhan's second-in-command. There were those who disapproved of an American holding such a high position, but there was no one else Reyhan trusted at his back.

"The royal family has a centuries-old relationship with the nomads," Reyhan said. "Under normal circumstances, I would agree to your plan to simply round them all up and let them rot in prison for a decade or so. But the majority of these boys are sons of chiefs, and I have given my word that I will not endanger them without cause. Threats are not cause."

"As you wish."

The tall, blond American rose to his feet and headed to his tent. Reyhan watched him go. Will was frustrated, but he wouldn't say any more. Instead he would do his job. He would focus on the task. Did he know a way to keep a man from going insane?

Reyhan closed his eyes and tried to see nothing, but instead Emma filled his mind. Being apart from her had only made him want her more. She was like water to a man dying of thirst. Her light filled his day and without her, he was blind.

Not much longer, he told himself, looking for comfort and finding none. Just a few more days and Emma would be gone. Then he would be free to marry someone else. A sensible woman who would bear him fine sons. A woman he could respect and never love. A woman who was not Emma.

Emma found use for one of her fancy dresses two nights later when she was invited to dine with the king, Cleo and her husband, Prince Jefri and Murat, the crown prince of Bahania. Nerves rode a roller coaster through her stomach as she carefully applied her makeup, and she wished Reyhan was going to be around. With him at her side, she would find it a whole lot easier to make casual conversation with everyone else at the table. But she hadn't heard from him since he'd left and she was beginning to think she wasn't going to.

What if the two weeks ended while he was gone and she had to leave Bahania without seeing him again? She briefly closed her eyes and told herself not to think about it. If she had to leave without seeing him again, she would survive. Maybe it would even help her get over him more quickly.

Not that she had anything to recover from. It's not as if she was falling for him or anything.

After checking the mirror one last time and smoothing the front of the peach-colored cocktail dress she'd pulled on, she walked out of the suite toward Cleo's rooms. Cleo and her husband had offered to escort her to the dinner so she wouldn't get lost on the way.

"This is Sadik," Cleo said a few minutes later as she introduced her husband.

Emma wasn't sure if she was expected to curtsy or what. Wishing she'd asked Cleo in advance, she held out her hand and tried to look more impressed than nervous. "Your Highness."

Sadik—tall, darkly handsome and more than a little intimidating—smiled. "As you are a member of the family, I suspect first names would be allowed." He bent slightly and kissed the back of her hand. "Welcome, Emma. I'm not sure how you have been able to put up with my brother these past few days, but the fact that you have is a testament to your character."

She'd been expecting to shake hands, so the kiss startled her, although not as much as the gentle teasing. Were all the princes *nice* as well as good-looking and powerful? Was it possible?

"He's been very kind," she murmured.

"But a fool. Any man who leaves such a beautiful wife on her own takes his chances."

Cleo, lush and amazing in a dark blue low-cut gown, raised her eyebrows. "Sadik, are you flirting?"

He turned to her. "I am making our new sister feel welcome. You know there is but one woman in my world."

He spoke with an intensity and love that made Emma feel she'd stumbled into a private moment. She turned away, but not before she saw the way Cleo smiled at her husband. It was a smile of true contentment and security. In that moment Emma vowed she would find a man who would love her as Sadik loved his wife, and she would give her whole heart to him.

The three of them walked into the hallway.

"Jefri's fun," Cleo said, linking arms with Emma. "He's the youngest and has a great sense of humor. Murat is more stuffy. I guess it's the whole crown prince thing."

"Murat has many responsibilities," Sadik said firmly. "The weight of the country rests on his shoulders."

"He's also still single," Cleo told her. "Imagine marrying him."

"No, thanks. I'm having trouble dealing with being a princess, however temporarily. I wouldn't want to think about being queen."

"Someone's going to have to," Cleo said. "The king has started talking about Murat needing an heir. Not that there aren't hundreds of women lining up to volunteer."

"She will be the mother of his sons," Sadik said. "Not a choice to be made lightly."

"Exactly," Cleo said with a grin. "Now, if he was going to only have daughters, then he could pretty much marry anyone."

Sadik sighed. "You mock me, wife."

"Pretty much every chance I get." She looked at Emma. "It's a hobby."

Emma was still chuckling when they walked into the formal dining room. This was not the same dining room she'd been in on her second night in Bahania.

That room had been impressive, but small and intimate. This one was much larger, with arched windows and elegant tapestries.

The table itself would seat at least twelve, and judging by the chairs lined up along one wall, could expand to seat many more. The inlaid wood gleamed in the soft light of crystal and gold chandeliers. The floor was marble, the flatware gold and the plates appeared hand painted and antique. Equally impressive, there wasn't a cat to be seen.

Despite the warm temperature outside, the room was cool and a fire crackled in a massive carved fireplace. The king stood beside it, a drink in his hand. Two men stood next to him. They were both tall and dark, with strong features and lean bodies.

Do they know how to grow handsome princes here or what? Emma thought, trying not to give in to her nerves and panic. She just had to get through the dinner, then she could escape back to her room. No biggie. Besides, if Jefri and Murat were as well mannered as Reyhan and Sadik, she would be made to feel welcome. There was nothing to worry about. Really.

Emma had nearly convinced herself when the king turned and saw them. As he approached, she felt her knees begin knocking together. Telling herself over and over that he was just a man didn't help. Not even a little.

"Emma," King Hassan said as he approached. "How lovely to see you."

He squeezed her arm lightly, then turned to Cleo, whom he kissed, then Sadik. The two men shook hands.

"I heard you went to our marketplace earlier this week," the king said as he led her to the other princes. "Did you enjoy it?"

"Very much. The people were gracious and kind."

"A Bahanian trait," he told her, then he introduced her to his sons.

They were much like Reyhan, yet different. Murat was taller and more serious. Jefri smiled easily. Both welcomed her.

When a servant approached to take her drink order, Emma chose white wine because she didn't want to appear out of place, but she had no intention of actually drinking any liquor. Not under these circumstances. Back home her friends teased her about being a complete lightweight, which was true. One drink and she was giggly, two and the world got blurry. Better to keep her wits about her tonight.

"It is unfortunate Reyhan couldn't be with us," Murat said a few minutes later.

Emma noticed the king in conversation with Sadik and Cleo while Jefri had excused himself to take a quick call from America. Something to do with the new Bahania Air Force. She smiled at the crown prince.

"Another familiar face in this impressive gathering would be helpful," she admitted. "But he has responsibilities and I understand that."

"Many women do not."

"I can't imagine why not."

"They find reasons." He sipped his drink as he studied her. "Is it true you knew nothing of who he was?"

"Absolutely. I didn't completely believe it even after I was brought here. The whole prince thing isn't exactly a part of my regular life."

"The life you will return to in a few days?"

She nodded.

"Regrets?" he asked.

She considered the question. "One or two foolish ones."

"Why foolish?"

She motioned to the room. "This is fifteen light-years from where I belong. Reyhan needs to find a wife who will fit into his world."

"You let him go easily."

Was Murat criticizing or stating the obvious? "It's what he wants."

"And what do you want?"

Emma thought of her time with Reyhan. How he'd made her laugh and made her ache. Of how her heart fluttered when he was in the room. Of how innocent she had been all those years ago and how she'd let him walk away.

"I would like to go back and do things differently."

"Not possible," he told her. "Not even for a prince."

Jefri returned just then and dinner was announced.

Emma found herself seated on the king's left, with Prince Jefri next to her. Murat was across from her. She felt the sharp gaze of the crown prince settle on her more than once as the appetizers were served. She longed to ask what he was thinking and if he would say anything to Reyhan when he returned. Were the brothers close? Did they confide in each other? Did Murat know something of Reyhan's heart, and if he did, would that information please her or hurt her?

"The planes are being delivered next week," Jefri said, sounding pleased.

"All that training will finally pay off," the king said. "Are they being delivered to El Bahar, as well?"

Jefri nodded. "The people from Van Horn will be here by the end of the month to start the integration process."

Cleo leaned toward Emma. "Okay, you look confused. El Bahar and Bahania are starting a joint air force to protect the oil fields. Jefri, who has been a flying fool for years, is in charge. He bought a bunch of really fast planes. F-somethings. Anyway, Van Horn Enterprises is a private firm that trains fighter pilots."

Sadik sighed. "I'm not sure where to start, Cleo."

She straightened. "What? Did I get any of it wrong?"

Jefri looked at her. "You called me a flying fool."

"And?"

One corner of his mouth twitched. "Never mind."

King Hassan looked indulgently at Cleo. "She has given me my first grandchild. Little else matters."

Cleo winked. "You gotta like that, right?"

Emma nodded, thinking that they might be royal and rich and live in a palace, but at heart this was a family like every other. The knot in her stomach untied and faded away.

Conversation turned to current events and how they

impacted Bahania. Emma had long known that Bahania was an American ally, but she was surprised by the close relationship the king and Murat obviously had with the president and several leaders in the Senate.

They had just been served a delicious chicken dish when one of the servants approached the king and spoke into his ear. The monarch listened, said something back, then looked at Emma.

"It seems there has been a slight plumbing problem in your suite," he said. "A pipe cracked and flooded the room. Nothing of yours was damaged, but you'll need to spend the night somewhere else." He smiled. "I think we can find a spare bed."

She thought of the dozens of rooms in the guest section. "I'm not concerned about it."

"Good. I have asked for your belongings to be packed and moved. After dinner I'll escort you to your new quarters myself."

"Thank you."

The meal lasted another two hours. When it was over, Emma felt so full, she could barely move. The king made good on his word and walked her to her new room.

"I hope you're enjoying your stay in my country," the monarch said as they turned a corner and started down a long corridor.

"Very much. What I've seen is so beautiful. And everyone has been so kind."

"Even my son?"

She glanced at him. He was tall, with a slight graying at his temple. In his dark suit he looked both regal and powerful.

"Especially Reyhan."

"I was sorry he could not dine with us tonight."

Emma agreed, but didn't want to say that. "He has responsibilities."

"He takes them seriously," King Hassan said. "As do all my sons. But in Reyhan's case, perhaps too seriously."

She wasn't sure what he meant, but before she could figure out a polite way to ask, they stopped in front of a large door.

"You will be staying in here," her host told her. "I hope you will find the room to your liking." He smiled and left.

Emma opened the door and stepped inside. The quarters were larger than her own had been, but more spartan. There were no overstuffed sofas and lush paintings. Instead the room was filled with simply designed pieces in muted earth tones and the artwork leaned more toward sculptures with a few boldly colored abstracts for contrast.

She turned on several lamps and walked around the living room. Something about it made her feel…not uneasy, just odd. The room was almost familiar. How strange. Had she seen it when she and Reyhan had toured the palace? She didn't remember any guest rooms being on their tour. Had she seen one similar?

She walked into the bedroom. The huge bed rested on a platform. Massive pieces of furniture filled the space without crowding her. Again the colors were muted but not—

She froze in place. There was a book on a night-stand. An open book. Quickly she crossed to the closet and pulled at the double doors. Dark suits lined one side of the closet. Built-in shelves were home to shirts, sweaters and shoes. Her own newly purchased wardrobe filled the other side of the closet. She fingered the sleeve of the closest suit and knew exactly who owned it.

Reyhan.

The king had moved her in with her husband.

Emma sighed, not sure what to do with the information. Should she protest? Request another room? Was King Hassan testing her? Testing them? Even with Reyhan gone, she felt that she didn't belong in his rooms. They had never lived as man and wife. This felt too…intimate.

In the bathroom she found her cosmetics on the same counter as his shaver. Two bathrobes hung by the large glassed-in shower. As if they had always been together.

Not sure what to do, Emma decided she would stay the night, then speak with Cleo in the morning. Perhaps the other woman would know what was going on and what Emma should do about it. In the meantime, she would simply pretend all this was real and that this was where she belonged.

Reyhan arrived back at the palace shortly after midnight. The same demons that had driven him away had forced him to return. He had to see her, touch her, breathe the same air she breathed. The need inside of him had grown until he couldn't eat or sleep. He could only *want*.

He took the stairs two at a time. When he reached the second floor, he walked toward the guest wing. But as he approached her door, he slowed his step until he stopped several feet away.

What was he going to do? Break down the door and take her? He closed his eyes and shook his head. No. He would be strong. Just a few more days and she would be gone. He was back in the palace now. Within a few feet of her. That would be enough. He would retreat to the safety of his own rooms and figure out a way to survive until she was gone.

Retracing his steps, he made his way to the other side of the building and let himself into his suite. He shrugged out of his jacket and left it on the back of the sofa. As he loosened his tie, he walked into the bedroom, only to come to a complete stop.

He was not alone.

A woman lay in his bed. In the moonlight streaming in from the open French doors he could see a bare arm, the curve of a cheek and dark hair tangled on a white pillow.

His heart stopped for a full second, then resumed at a thundering pace. His body heated as blood raced down to his groin. He was instantly hard and ready to take.

Emma was in his bed.

Chapter Eight

Reyhan told himself to leave, to back out of the room before she awoke. As much as he wanted her, he couldn't have her. Not now, not ever. But he couldn't move. The passion was too strong. He could only stand in place and drink in her beauty.

He must have made a sound, or perhaps she sensed his presence, because she stirred, turned over then opened her eyes.

"Reyhan?" she asked, her voice sleepy. She pushed her hair out of her face and raised herself on one elbow. "What time is it?" She glanced at the clock, then back at him. "I've only been asleep for a couple of seconds. I thought…" She blinked. "Wait. What are you doing here?"

"This is my room."

"What?" She glanced around. "Oh." Her breath caught. "*Oh!* Right. I, ah, I had dinner with the king and your family and while we were eating someone came and told him that a pipe had broken in my suite. So he said he would put me somewhere else. Which turned out to be here. I thought it was weird, but it was late and I figured I would just stay here until morning, then straighten it out. I didn't think you'd be back tonight."

Of course she didn't. He hadn't told her when he would return. But he'd told his father who had most likely arranged for him to find Emma sleeping in his bed. While he was curious as to why his father wanted to tempt him with Emma, he was more concerned about the temptation itself. He had to get out of here before he said or did something he would regret. Before he gave in to the hunger consuming him.

"I'm sorry," she said, sitting up and drawing her knees to her chest. "I should have said something right away. I can go find somewhere else to sleep."

She started to climb out of the bed. He caught a glimpse of semitransparent fabric and sensuous curves.

"Don't," he said, turning away and staring blindly out the French doors. "Just stay there. I'll leave."

"But this is your room."

"Tonight it is yours."

Tonight and always, he thought, knowing he would never forget seeing her there. In the morning, when she was gone, he would haunt the rooms, searching for some hint of her presence, some clue that she'd been there at all.

"How were your meetings?" she asked.

"They went well."

"Did you really have to go, or were you just avoiding me?"

The softly worded question surprised him. The Emma he remembered would never have been so bold. He returned his attention to her and found her sitting cross-legged, staring at the sheets.

"I was avoiding you, but not for the reasons you think."

Her chin lifted and her eyes widened. "I don't understand."

Perhaps it was the night. Perhaps it was the ache inside of him, an ache that grew and fed on his soul. Perhaps it was the hint of sweetness in the air, the scent of which could only come from Emma. Perhaps it was madness. Regardless of the reason, he decided to speak the truth.

"I cannot be around you without wanting you," he said. "Rather than give in, I went away."

Understanding dawned slowly. The soft light of the moon didn't allow him to see her blush, but he imagined it. She swallowed, then shrugged.

"Oh. I, ah…" She cleared her throat. "You mean sex."

Her acceptance nearly made him smile. He wasn't sure if she was trying to act casually or if she was truly unsurprised by his admission. What had she learned in their six years apart and who had been her teacher?

"I prefer to think of it as making love, but, yes."

She tucked her hair behind her ears. "I guess it's

a guy thing," she said. "I never understood all the fuss."

He did his best not to react to her words, not to hope too much. "Your lovers have not pleased you?"

Her nose wrinkled. "I've sort of avoided the whole man-in-my-bed thing. It's not my style."

Two warring thoughts invaded his brain and produced two very different reactions. First was pleasure and relief that she hadn't been with anyone else. That she was still only his. The second was stung pride that he hadn't satisfied her when they'd been together. He knew now that he'd been too intent on his own release, on claiming her over and over. He hadn't taken the time to pleasure her.

"Not that it's your fault," she said, interrupting his internal battle. "I was too young. We went from kissing, to, well, you know, too fast for me. You were right about what you said before, that I wanted a schoolgirl's courtship with kisses and presents."

So hard that he thought he might explode, Reyhan forced himself to walk to the chair close to the bed and sit down.

"You were a virgin," he told her. "That fault lies with me. I was young and eager to take my bride. Too eager."

She ducked her head again. "Yes, well, it happens."

"It should not have happened that way. The women I had been with before had been older and more experienced. They had been the teacher and I the student. With you…" He clenched his teeth. "I should have been more patient, more understanding.

I should have seduced you with slow kisses and soft touches. Only when you were begging for more should I have taken you.''

A shudder rippled through her body. ''That sounds nice,'' she whispered.

The slight quaver in her voice told him she was not unaffected by his words. The knowledge nearly propelled him to his feet and across the room to the bed. What would happen if he slid in beside her? Would she welcome him? Want him? Respond to him? Every cell in his body screamed for him to find out.

No! He could not. He knew the price of being with her again. A single moment of exquisite pleasure followed by a lifetime of wanting what he could not have. Better to not have her at all.

He forced himself to stand but not approach, and nearly shook with the intensity of his feelings. ''Good night, Emma,'' he said as he turned away. ''Sleep well.''

''Reyhan, wait.''

A rustle of sheets told him she had slid out of the bed. Her footsteps made no noise on the thick carpet but he *felt* her approach.

His blood boiled, his erection throbbed. It was more than he could bear and yet he did not turn around. He would not do this. No matter how much resisting cost him.

''Before,'' she whispered, her voice low and husky. ''When you kissed me. It was different.''

He thought of her passion, of how she'd clung to him, demanding as much as he. They'd fit together perfectly. Everything about her had called to him, yet he'd forced himself to pull back.

"It *was* different," he agreed.

"I'm not that child anymore."

Five simple words—an invitation to paradise.

He heard them and was nearly afraid to believe.

It doesn't matter, he told himself desperately. Taking her now, making love with her, would be a disaster. How would he let her go? How would he marry someone he didn't care about and live with her for the rest of his life? What of his future, his plans? What of being strong?

What of Emma?

Without thought, he turned slowly and stared at her. She stood only a few feet away, naked except for the diaphanous silk nightgown skimming her curves. Her long auburn hair tumbled over her shoulders; the curling ends lightly teased the tops of her breasts. Her eyes were bright, her lips slightly parted, her breathing rapid.

He told himself he could still resist her, and he nearly believed himself. Until she walked closer, raised herself on tiptoe and pressed her mouth to his.

The soft, gentle, chaste pressure undid him. It was as if the savage beast inside had been set free to prey upon the world. He grabbed her and pulled her close, wanting to touch everywhere at once. As his mouth settled on hers, he rubbed her back, her hips, then her fanny. He could feel the smoothness of her skin under the thin gown, but it wasn't enough. He needed more.

Tilting his head, he swept his tongue across her lower lip. When she parted for him, he plunged inside, stroking, exploring, needing. At the same time he tugged on the fabric of her gown, pulling it higher and higher until it bunched in his left hand. With his right, he stroked the now-bare skin of her hips, then slid up her back. She shivered and wrapped her arms around him.

He ground himself against her, rubbing his arousal against her belly. She flexed into him and moaned softly.

He let the nightgown fall back to her ankles and raised his hands to her shoulders. The thin straps slid down easily. He moved from her mouth to her jaw, then her neck, tasting her skin, licking, sucking, nipping. He bathed her long, slender neck with sensual attentions that made her shudder and cling to him. He bit her shoulder, then licked the wound.

The silk clung to her breasts, but one quick tug drew the fabric over her tight nipples so that it fluttered to the floor. Then she was naked.

Torn between looking and touching, he bent down and took her nipple in his mouth. He circled his tongue around the hard peak and she groaned her pleasure. She wrapped one arm around his shoulders and the other around his neck. Her fingers tunneled through his hair.

"Reyhan," she breathed. "It's too good. All of it."

Her words were like icy water thrown in his face. Reality crashed in on him as he realized what he was doing. Taking her hard and fast. They weren't even in bed. He was still fully dressed. Had he learned nothing?

Reyhan swore under his breath, which didn't bother

Emma nearly as much as when he stopped what he'd been doing. He straightened, leaving her nipples damp and achy. Everywhere he'd touched, she burned. Tension tightened her muscles and made her tremble. She didn't even mind that she was naked—not as long as he kept touching her.

"I'm sorry," he breathed.

She stared at him, at his dilated dark eyes and the firm set of his mouth. "For what? I liked it."

One corner of his mouth pulled up in a smile. "I'm glad you liked it but my plan was to seduce, not take."

"Taking works. Really."

"That is because you haven't been seduced. Come. I will show you the difference."

He led her to the bed and urged her to lie down. While she made herself comfortable, he quickly stripped out of his clothes, leaving only the briefs covering his arousal. Her interest in the long, hard bulge dissipated when he slid in next to her and pulled her close.

"You are so beautiful," he whispered into her ear right before he took the lobe between his teeth and nibbled.

Shivers rippled across her skin.

"You're soft," he continued as he kissed below her ear, then down her throat. One of his hands lightly stroked her belly.

"The scent of your skin drives me wild with passion. I ache to be inside of you. Filling you slowly, deeply, until your pleasure makes you scream your delight."

Scream? She didn't consider herself the type. But under the circumstances, she was willing to give it a try. Just the feel of his hand on her belly made her want to squirm. Up or down, she thought as he kissed her jaw. He needed to move that hand either up or down. Having it right there in the middle was making her crazy.

"The color of your nipples," he whispered. "Like a fully ripe peach. Open your eyes."

The unexpected request took a second to sink in. Emma opened her eyes and saw Reyhan lean over her breasts. As she watched, he touched the tip of his tongue to the tip of her left nipple. The combination of seeing and feeling was the most erotic experience of her life. She cried out in delight.

He circled her nipple, then drew it fully into his mouth. The gentle sucking had her arching against him. At the same time, his hand finally dipped south, slipping through her curls and between her legs.

She parted for him, catching her breath as he rubbed against her slick center.

This was nothing like before, she thought as tension filled her body. She ached with every fiber of her being. When he shifted his fingers slightly and found a single spot of pleasure, she nearly rose off the bed.

"Reyhan," she breathed. "Don't stop."

Thankfully, he didn't. He continued to touch her, stroking her, teasing, circling, as he worshiped her breasts. The combination made her mind go blank, her legs go limp and her breathing come in fast pants.

She couldn't bear herself enough to him. She wanted to be more naked, more exposed, more intimate.

Her wish was granted when he shifted so that he knelt between her legs and kissed his way down her belly. Part of her suspected what he was going to do while the rest of her couldn't believe it was really happening. She'd heard…she'd read…but before, he'd never…

He kissed her between her legs—an openmouthed kiss that made her tremble. Tension exploded inside of her as muscles tensed and collected. He found that one spot and licked it over and over until all she could do was dig her heels into the mattress and clutch the sheets with her hands. She tossed her head from side to side, tried to catch her breath, then gave up air completely as her release claimed her.

She hadn't known, she thought hazily as her body released and muscles contracted, that this much pleasure existed in the world. That she could feel so good, so right, so everything.

Her climax rippled through her and still he touched her, gentling the contact until the last drop had been wrung from her body. She opened her eyes and stared at him.

"I can't believe you did that."

He smiled. "Better than before."

"Miraculous. I've never…" She wiggled, feeling more than a little self-conscious. "You know."

"Yes, I know."

He sat up and removed his briefs. She barely had time to gaze at his arousal before he settled between her legs and kissed her breasts. She felt a shivery kind of ache all over. Suddenly there were more possibilities than she'd ever realized and she wanted him inside of her.

"Yes," she whispered, as he raised his head and stared at her. "Be in me." She reached between them and guided him inside.

He was large and stretched her in the best way possible. She felt filled, yet the need for more grew.

He wrapped his arms around her, drawing her close so they pressed together everywhere. She clung to him, urging him deeper.

"More," she breathed as he withdrew only to fill her again.

The rhythmic thrusting made her pulse against him. She couldn't get enough and she couldn't seem to keep control. She strained toward him, reaching, needing, wanting. She dropped her hands to his hips to pull him closer.

"Take me," she begged. "Oh, Reyhan, yes."

In and out, in and out. Tension grew again. She couldn't focus on anything but what they were doing. And then her body convulsed in release and she could only hang on as he took her to heaven and back. At the very end, when she was sure there couldn't be anything else, he shuddered in her embrace and called out her name.

Later, when the moon had set and they were both lying naked under the covers, Emma rested her head on Reyhan's shoulder. He was warm and relaxed next to her. She had the thought that things could have been awkward between them, but he'd made everything so easy and right by simply pulling her close.

As if he never planned on letting her go and this was exactly where she belonged.

Emma awoke to a bright sunny day and the feeling that she could quite possibly fly. As she lay in the large bed and relived her night with Reyhan, she felt herself smiling, tingling and fighting the urge to break out in song.

So *that* was what all the fuss was about, she thought happily as she rubbed her hand against the sheets where Reyhan had slept. Amazing how she'd missed the whole point before. Now she got it completely. Her only regret was that he hadn't taken her again and again, as he had on their honeymoon. For the first time, making love several times a day made perfect sense.

"We'll have tonight," she said as she tossed back the covers and stood. She was still naked, but there wasn't anyone around to see. After grabbing her robe from the foot of the bed, she walked into the bathroom and turned on the shower.

As she stepped into the steaming spray, she had the thought that night was really far off and maybe he wasn't doing anything for lunch. Or there was that massive desk in his office. The surface might be a little hard, but the space had possibilities. She was still laughing when she began to shampoo her hair.

Forty minutes later she made her way through the hallways of the palace. She found Reyhan's office with only a single wrong turn and practically beamed at the man in the foyer.

"Princess Emma," he said, leaping to his feet. "I'll tell your husband you're here."

"Thank you."

Emma continued to smile at no one in particular and practically floated into Reyhan's office. He hung up the phone as she entered.

"Is there a problem?" he asked, sounding both distant and stern.

"No. Of course not." She paused expectantly and waited.

He stared at her. A grandfather clock in the corner ticked. The silence grew.

She felt some of her happiness bleed away, and with the sensation came the chilling thought that he had regrets about what had happened.

After a few seconds, he rose and circled around his desk. "I'm very busy, Emma. Is there something you need?"

He spoke almost coldly, as if she were an assistant who had lingered too long. Trepidation clutched at her chest and she took a step back.

"I thought…" She swallowed. "I was just…" Mentioning her fantasy of a lunch break on his desk seemed impossible.

Who was this distant stranger? she wondered frantically. Where was the hotly passionate man from the previous night? What had happened?

He waited, watching her, giving nothing away. She remembered then that he'd tried to leave the bedroom and she'd been the one to stop him. Had she kept him against his will? Had he not wanted to make love with her? Had he done it out of obligation?

Her eyes began to burn but she refused to give in to tears. She was all grown up now, and she'd known what she was doing when she'd invited him into her bed. She *wanted* to make love with him. If there were consequences, they were her responsibility.

Pride squared her shoulders and raised her chin. She met his dark gaze. Maybe this was the moment to get answers to her questions.

"Why did you ever marry me?" she asked. "And once you decided to return to Bahania, why did you *stay* married to me? I don't believe it was because you were afraid to tell your father what you'd done. You fear no man."

"It doesn't matter."

"Maybe not to you but I want to know what's going on. You disappeared from my life for years, then you dragged me back here, played the charming host, then disappeared. Last night—"

A knock on the closed door interrupted her.

Reyhan frowned. "What is it?" he called.

His assistant stepped into the room. "I'm sorry, sir. I wouldn't have disturbed you except you and Princess Emma have been summoned by the king. He wishes to see both of you right away. It seems her parents have arrived at the palace."

"They can't be here," Emma murmured as she and Reyhan walked through the maze of corridors. "They don't like to fly. They never wanted me to. All our vacations were by car."

But here they were. As she followed Reyhan into a large reception room, she saw her parents standing with the king in an obviously awkward moment of silence.

When she came to a stop, Reyhan paused beside her. So far, he hadn't said anything, and she was grateful. This was going to be difficult enough without him taking on her family for withholding significant information from her for years.

In the second before they looked up and saw her, she studied them. Her mother was small and a little bent, her thick hair more gray than red, her father much taller and spare. They looked old, frail and out of place. Funny how all her life they'd seemed so powerful. She'd been afraid to defy them, to question the rules. Her only act of rebellion had been to fall in love with Reyhan and then run off with him, and she'd paid for that several times over. Now she saw they were just people. Older, out of their element and afraid for her. They had acted out of love, however misplaced, taking control because she'd never told them they shouldn't.

"Emma!" her mother shouted as she saw her. Both her parents rushed over and hugged her fiercely. Reyhan moved away.

"Are you all right?" her father asked. "Have they hurt you?"

"What? I'm fine. Everyone has treated me exceptionally well." She thought about last night. *Well* didn't begin to describe it.

"You shouldn't have left Dallas," her mother said as she brushed at Emma's sleeve. "You know you're not strong. Situations like this confuse you."

"I would think finding out you're a princess would

confuse anyone," Emma said, trying to step back, but they held on tight.

Flanking her, they turned to the king. "We've filed an official complaint with the State Department protesting our daughter's kidnapping," her father said.

"Dad, no. I wasn't kidnapped. I'm here as the king's guest to deal with my marriage to Reyhan. You're seriously overreacting."

"Am I?" He looked at her. "You up and disappeared, you lied to us about where you'd gone. For all we know, they're brainwashing you."

From the corner of her eye she saw Reyhan take a step forward. Outrage darkened his features. She didn't want to think about how much her father had just insulted the king.

"I'm not being brainwashed," she said, then realized it was a foolish argument. If she was, would she know?

"As your daughter's husband, it is my duty to care for her," Reyhan said stiffly. "I assure you, her safety and well-being are my primary concern."

"Some concern," her mother said tartly. "You're the reason she's here in the first place. If you hadn't carted her off back then none of this would have happened. She was just a child."

"I was eighteen," Emma reminded her. "I loved him."

"You don't know what love is," her mother told her, still glaring at Reyhan.

"You seduced her and then ran off," her father added. "What kind of concern is that?"

Reyhan glared at the older man. "I attempted to

contact her on several occasions. You're the ones who kept me from her.''

''Good thing we did. Who knows what would have happened if we hadn't?''

She would have come to Bahania, Emma thought. She would have been Reyhan's wife. They would have had children.

''This isn't accomplishing anything,'' she told her parents. ''I married Reyhan and now we all have to deal with it. I don't want you interfering. You already got between us once. It won't happen again.''

Her mother stared at her. ''You said you were here to get a divorce.''

''I am, but—''

''Then there's nothing to get in the way of, is there?''

''No, but—''

Her mother narrowed her gaze. ''We'll be taking our daughter with us this afternoon. If you would have someone pack up her things.''

''I'm not leaving,'' Emma said. ''Not yet.''

''Why not?'' her father wanted to know. ''You can't possibly plan to—''

''Silence,'' the king said.

His voice wasn't especially loud, but something in the tone got everyone's attention. They all turned to him.

He smiled at her parents. ''You are my honored guests for as long as you would like to stay in Bahania. Or you may leave at any time, as may your daughter.''

That surprised her. Reyhan also looked startled.

"The divorce," he said.

His father nodded. "That is a separate matter." The monarch paused.

Emma felt her inside clench in panic. Suddenly she didn't want to hear what King Hassan had to say. Was he granting the divorce a few days early? It made the most sense, but she didn't want him to. Things were too unsettled between herself and Reyhan. She needed to understand what last night had meant and why he'd been so cold this morning. She wanted to know what the fluttering when he was near meant. Was it just about sexual attraction or was there more?

Time. She needed time.

The king looked at her and it was as if he could read her mind. His kind eyes seemed to tell her that everything would be all right. To trust him. She took a deep breath and tried to relax.

"Despite Reyhan's request for a divorce, I am not convinced it is the right course of action," the king said.

"No!" her mother protested.

"This is an outrage," her father said.

Reyhan was completely silent and Emma felt only a sense of relief.

"It is my decision that Reyhan and Emma must get to know each other again. Something drew them together enough for them to impulsively marry. Was it a youthful prank or true love? Only time will tell. Therefore they must spend two months in each other's company. Not a day or a night apart. At the end of that time we will speak again. If they still both wish to divorce, I will grant it and their marriage will disappear as if it had never been."

Chapter Nine

Emma felt both relief and panic at the king's proclamation. Two months in Reyhan's company. If there were more nights like the previous one, that would hardly be difficult duty.

She glanced at the man who had married her. It was as if his expression were made of stone. She couldn't tell what he was thinking, nor could she see anything friendly or welcoming in his dark eyes. One thing she *was* sure of—he didn't look happy.

Without saying anything, Reyhan turned and left the room. Emma watched him go and tried to ignore the knot that returned to her stomach.

Beside her, her parents continued to protest.

''There has to be some legal court we can take this up with,'' her father said heatedly.

The king appeared more amused than insulted. "Mr. and Mrs. Kennedy, please." He opened his arms in a gesture of welcome. "You are honored guests in my country. I would ask you to stay here in the palace as long as you would like. Visit with your daughter. Get to know my people. You will find things very pleasant. As for your daughter—" he smiled at Emma "—she is a charming young woman. You must be very proud."

Her mother sniffed. "Of course we are. She's a very good girl."

Emma felt like a wayward puppy who had finally been pronounced housebroken.

"I do not wish to be unreasonable." The king turned to her father. "You are right—there are courts and laws. They state all royal marriages must be approved by the king. Reyhan defied me when he married your lovely daughter. Having met Emma, I can forgive his impulsiveness. Who could blame him?"

While she appreciated the compliment, she thought he was laying it on a little thick.

"This isn't her world," her mother said. "She belongs home, with us."

"She is a grown woman. Perhaps it is time for *her* to say where she belongs. In two months she will have that opportunity."

He beckoned someone from the rear of the room. Emma saw several servants approaching.

"Show the Kennedys to their quarters," he said, then nodded and left.

Emma's mother huffed. "Just like that. You have a life. Has he forgotten that? Responsibilities. A job."

Emma blinked in surprise. Honestly, she'd forgotten all about that. Her world back home. Funny how it had faded from her memory so quickly.

"You're right. I'll have to take a leave of absence."

"They won't like that," her father told her. "You've not even been working there a year."

Good point. "I'll have to explain things," she said, not sure how she was going to. Would anyone believe her? "If I do get fired, I'll find another job when I get home."

"A very cavalier attitude," her mother said. "You were raised better than that."

"Mom, I know you're worried. I appreciate that, and I know you only came here because you care about me. But I'm twenty-four. It's time to let me live my life my own way. If I make mistakes, then I'll recover from them."

Her mother's mouth dropped open, while her father seemed equally surprised. She took advantage of the silence and smiled at one of the servants.

"Okay," she said. "Lead the way." She linked arms with her parents. "You two are going to love this place. The rooms are amazing. And the views, even better than when we went to Galveston my senior year of high school."

Her mother sighed. "I don't like any of this, Emma. It's not you."

"I know. But from what I can tell, I don't have a choice. The king has to give his permission for a prince to get a divorce. So I'm stuck here until that happens."

Two months with Reyhan. What would that time bring? Would she learn to understand the man she'd married so impulsively? Would she be eager to leave when the time was up? Or would she find herself falling in love? And if it was the latter, would he love her back or would he still want to get rid of her so he could marry someone else?

Reyhan didn't return to his offices. Instead he walked to the garages where he took the keys for a Jeep and drove out of the city. An hour later, surrounded by desert, he stepped out into the warm afternoon and raised his face to the sky.

He wanted to yell his frustration, to rip and tear something. Anything. He wanted to travel north, deep into the inhospitable land and become someone else.

Two months. It was an eternity. How could he survive spending his days and nights with her? How could he be close to her and not reach for her?

Last night had been paradise. A miracle. When he'd left her bed this morning all he'd been able to think about was how much he wanted her. Having her had only increased his need. When she'd walked into his office, he'd held on to his control with every ounce of will he possessed. Just a few minutes longer and he would have snapped.

"I am Prince Reyhan of Bahania," he yelled to the heavens. "I am a man of power, of substance."

Yet in the presence of a mere woman he was weak. He would travel any distance, complete any task, risk life, limb anything, just for Emma.

He clutched the side of the Jeep. There had to be

a solution somewhere. An answer, a trick, a way to survive two months around her without going mad. He couldn't give in and take her into his bed. If he did, he would never let her go. And if she stayed…

He sucked in a breath as he considered the possibility. To have her stay was to love her. To give her his very soul. Then he would be nothing but a shell of a man. A spineless creature—a parasite.

No! That could never happen. Somehow he would conquer this. He would find the strength to turn away from her. To resist her. When the time was up, he would let her go. It was the only way. The alternative was unthinkable.

Emma went with her parents to the guest suite. It was similar to the one she'd had and even the ever sensible and conservative George and Janice Kennedy were impressed.

"You can see the ocean," her mother said as she stared out the large French doors.

"It's the Arabian Sea," Emma told her. "Bahania has some beautiful beaches. Tourism is an important industry."

Her father opened the suitcase one of the servants had left on the bed. "I can't believe they wanted to unpack for us. Like we're invalids or something."

"It's not that they thought you were incapable," Emma said. "It's part of the service."

"I've always done my own cooking and cleaning," her mother reminded her. "I never did understand those women who pay someone else to come in and clean their dirt. It's not right." Her mouth pressed together as tears filled her eyes. "None of this is right."

Emma took her hand and led her back into the large living room. Her father followed. When the two of them were seated on the sofa, she curled up in the wing chair across the glass-topped coffee table.

"We have to talk about it," she said.

Her mother pulled a lace-edged hankie out of her sleeve. "There's nothing to say. That man was trouble before and he's trouble now."

"Don't distress yourself, Janice," her father said gently. "We're here now and we'll make sure our girl is safe."

"I know. It's just… This place. It's so big and fancy."

"The palace is amazing," Emma said, trying not to get sucked into a familiar pattern of panic when she upset her parents. Knowing she made her mother cry was enough to give her a stomach ache for three days. But she couldn't keep giving in. King Hassan had been right when he'd said it was time for her to make some decisions about her life.

"All this is happening now because we didn't straighten things out six years ago," she said.

Her father sighed. "We went over this, kitten."

The familiar name made her stiffen. For years she's loved that he called her that, but now she wasn't so sure. A kitten was hardly a force to be reckoned with.

"You should have told me what was going on," she said quietly. "I had the right to know that Reyhan had tried to see me."

Her mother started to speak, but Emma held up her

hand to stop her. "If I was old enough to get married, I was old enough to know the truth."

"But you would have gone away with him," her mother wailed. "We would never have seen you."

"Is that what this was all about? Keeping me close?"

Her parents looked at each other, then at her. "We only wanted what was best for you," her father said. "We love you."

Why had she been afraid of defying them for so long? she wondered. They were just people. Misguided, maybe. She might not agree with their decision, but she believed they'd done what they thought was right. Their motivation had been selfish, but only because they cared about her.

"Emma, we should have said something about the money," her mother admitted. "It was such a large amount. It's not that Reyhan was bad, it's just that he wasn't like us. You were so sad. When you were happy again, we wanted to keep you that way."

Emma didn't know what to feel. Loss for what could have been. Although would she and Reyhan have had a chance all those years ago? At eighteen she'd barely been able to take care of herself. How would she have handled a husband, and maybe a child?

"It's done," she said, wanting to move on. "We can't change it and now we have a different situation to deal with."

Her mother sighed. "I can't believe the king is going to insist you stay here two months. That's barbaric."

Emma smiled. "You can call living in the palace a lot of things, but not that. Besides, I want a chance to get to know Reyhan again."

Her parents exchanged a look of worry and panic. "Is that such a good idea, kitten?" her father asked.

"I don't know. I loved him once."

"You were just a little girl."

"Legally, I was an adult," she said, silently admitting that on the inside she'd been a child. "But that's not the point. As King Hassan said, there's a reason the two of us ran off."

Her mother pressed her lips together. "We all know what *his* reason was. He was little more than an animal."

Emma thought of what had happened the previous night. A little more animal-like behavior would be fine with her.

"You two have loved each other for nearly fifty years. Don't you want that for me?"

"Not with him," her father said. "Can't you find a nice boy back home? Emma, you're only twenty-four. You have years before you have to settle down and get married."

"I'm already married. I'm staying the two months, and I'm going to take the time to get to know Reyhan again."

Her mother's eyes welled with tears. "But what if you fall in love with him?"

Would she? "It's a chance I'm willing to take."

"Oh, Emma. He broke your heart before. What's to stop him from doing it again?"

Good question. "I have to risk it. I'm sorry. I know

you want to protect me but this time you can't. I have to do it on my own. So I'm going to ask you to trust me.''

Her elderly parents stared at her. She sensed their misgivings and fear. Then they looked at each other and nodded.

''All right, kitten,'' her father said. ''If this is what you really want, we'll stand by your decision.''

''When he destroys you, we'll be here to pick up the pieces,'' her mother added. ''We'll take you home and you can move back into your own room.''

Talk about motivation to make things work with Reyhan, Emma thought. Still, she wouldn't let her parents sway her one way or the other. The king had granted her the gift of time and she intended to take advantage of it.

Emma spent the afternoon with her parents. She took them on a tour of the palace, the gardens and the chapel. They seemed to enjoy the dozens of cats more than anything. An hour before dinner, she returned to the room she now shared with Reyhan and called her supervisor back in Dallas. Fifteen minutes later she found herself on indefinite leave and accepting good wishes that it all work out for the best.

If only, she thought as she hung up the phone.

She leaned back on the sofa and tried to figure out what to do next. She was having dinner with her parents. There would be a more formal event with the king and several ministers the following evening, and a party later in the weekend.

''A whirlwind of social events,'' she murmured to

herself, trying not to feel nervous as she watched the clock and waited for Reyhan to return. However much he might want to avoid it, they *had* to talk, and the sooner the better.

Thirty minutes later, she'd given up trying to read her book. Sixty minutes later she was pacing the room with the intensity of an athlete training for an Olympic event. When the main door of the suite finally opened, Emma nearly stumbled in shock.

Elation, excitement and trepidation coiled together in her stomach as she searched Reyhan's face, hoping for a clue as to what he was thinking. There wasn't one.

"Good evening," he said when he saw her. "Are your parents settled?"

Not the words of a man overwhelmed by passion and desire, she thought sadly as she fought her own visceral reactions to being in the same room as the man who had taught her what all the fuss was about.

"Yes. They love their rooms." A slight exaggeration, but he was unlikely to press her. "How are you?"

"Fine."

He walked past her into the bedroom. She trailed after him, wishing he'd said a little more. "I'm having dinner with my parents tonight," she said. "You're welcome to come, but you don't have to. I know they probably make you uncomfortable."

Reyhan shrugged out of his suit jacket. "I would think the situation would be the reverse."

That he made them nervous? Probably. "Would you care to join us?" she asked. "Do you have to because of what the king said?'' Days *and* nights together. She still wasn't sure what that meant.

He loosened his tie. ''My father's statement was meant to keep me from taking an extended business trip. We are not required to spend every waking second in each other's company.''

Too bad. She twisted her hands together. ''I didn't know what to do about staying here. Should I? Do you want me to move to one of the guest rooms?''

Reyhan pulled his tie free of his shirt collar. ''No. Stay here. I'll sleep in the second bedroom.''

Supreme happiness crashed in and burned in a tenth of a second. ''There's another bedroom?'' she asked, because the alternative was to ask why he didn't want them to sleep together.

''I have a small office at the other end of the suite. I'll have a bed brought in. We'll have to share the living quarters and the bathroom, but I'll make every effort not to get in your way.''

''But I... But we...'' She swallowed and took a step toward him. ''Reyhan, what's going on? Why are you acting like this?''

He pulled his shirttail out of his trousers. Her gaze dropped to his belt and she had the sudden fantasy that he was going to get naked in front of her. Wouldn't that be a treat?

His expression turned weary. ''It is only two months,'' he said. ''Surely you can endure my company that long.''

''Enduring your company isn't the problem. Last night...'' She cleared her throat. ''Reyhan, we made love.''

He turned away and crossed to the French doors. "It will not happen again."

Stark words that clawed at her heart. "Because you don't want me?"

Because it wasn't good? Hadn't she pleased him? Last night she'd been so sure, but now...

Her throat tightened, as did her chest. Her legs felt heavy and thick, as if they belonged to someone else.

He bowed his head briefly. "Two months, Emma. That is all. At the end of that time, you can return to Texas where you belong."

And he would stay here, marry another woman and have children with her.

"But I thought..."

He turned to her. She'd never seen such coldness in a man's eyes before. Such rejection. "You thought wrong."

"I swear, there should be a law allowing wives of princes to lock their husbands in chains once a month. Just to keep them in line," Princess Sabrina said, grinning.

"Would you want to beat him, too?" Cleo asked as she reached for a slice of cantaloupe.

"Only when he really makes me crazy. Probably every third month."

"Works for me," Princess Zara said cheerfully. "Not that I'd ever want to hurt Rafe, but threatening him from time to time would make me really happy."

The three women laughed with delight. Emma smiled, knowing however big they talked, none of them was anything but completely in love with their husbands. She'd sensed it from the first moment they'd met.

Cleo had arrived that morning to invite her to lunch. "Without your folks," she'd insisted. "Not that they're not great, but you need a break."

Sabrina and Zara, both daughters of the king, although by different mothers, had been charming as they'd welcomed Emma.

"So you're the mystery woman Reyhan married," Sabrina said as she passed around a plate of tea sandwiches. She was seven or eight months pregnant and a beauty with dark eyes and dark brown hair highlighted with red.

Zara, equally pretty but in a more quiet way, looked like her sister. She was pregnant, as well, but not so far along.

"I don't consider myself a mystery," Emma said, which was true. Compared with being a princess, her life was pretty boring.

"Reyhan never said a word," Sabrina told her. "Not that any of my brothers are the chatty type. But a wife. That's a big secret to keep." She tilted her head and smile. "Then you appear out of the blue. Are you completely freaked?"

"Pretty much."

"I would be, too," Zara told her. "Sabrina grew up with all this, so she's used to it, but for the rest of us it's been a challenge."

Cleo laughed. "It's true. Zara resisted being a princess for the longest time."

"So did you," Zara reminded her.

"For different reasons. You were one by birth. Sa-dik wanted me to be one by marriage."

Emma was confused. "Didn't you want to marry him? You're so in love."

"It's complicated," Cleo told her. "A story for another time." She leaned over the back of the sofa in her suite and checked on Calah. "This is the best baby in the universe. She never cries, she sleeps like a dream and I swear she has an IQ of about two hundred."

Sabrina and Zara rolled their eyes. Emma laughed.

"She's *very* smart," Cleo said, sounding huffy. "You guys wait until your babies are born. You'll see what I mean."

"Sure, Cleo," Sabrina said. "I'm guessing we'll all be as goofy as you about our children."

"You mock me now, but just you wait."

"Watch yourself," Sabrina said to Emma. "There's something about this palace. It's pregnancy central. Be careful or you'll catch a baby of your own."

The three women laughed and Emma tried to join in, not that she was very successful. It was hard to joke when she'd just realized that she and Reyhan hadn't used protection when they'd made love.

She sucked in a breath and tried to stay calm. It had only been one time, she reminded herself. A quick calculation told her the day had been safe, rel-atively speaking. So she was unlikely to be pregnant. Based on how he was avoiding her, she wasn't going to be in a position to have a second chance at getting pregnant, either. Which was good. Right?

She *was* happy not to have to deal with an unexpected baby. Except she could easily picture herself with Reyhan's child. Holding him or her and overwhelmed by love. That would be wonderful.

She knew Reyhan wanted children, just not with her. Which made her wonder why. He'd been willing to marry her before. Why was he so determined *not* to be married to her now? She didn't think there was anyone else in his life. He'd said he would accept an arranged union. So she—

"Earth to Emma," Zara said. "Are you still with us?"

Emma blinked and saw all three women looking at her. "Sorry. I was lost in thought."

"I bet I know who was starring in that fantasy," Sabrina said teasingly. "It would be romantic if it wasn't my brother."

Emma felt herself coloring. "No, really. It was nothing."

As she'd never been a very good liar, she wasn't surprised when they didn't buy her story.

"Maybe there's more going on than we know about," Cleo said. "Which could be interesting."

"We'd love to have you as part of our princess sisterhood," Zara told her. "Think about it."

"Thanks."

She appreciated the invitation more than she could say. She'd always wanted a sister. But staying or not staying wasn't just up to her. Reyhan had a part in it, and based on what she'd seen so far, he couldn't wait to have her gone.

Chapter Ten

Two days later Emma accompanied her parents down to the stable. The king had suggested Reyhan take them out into the desert to show them some of Bahania's natural beauty. She was relatively sure her husband had agreed to the outing because he didn't have a choice. Ever since they'd shared that one night, he'd made it more than clear that spending time in her company was about as pleasant as root canal sugery.

What hurt her was that her feelings were so different. Since sharing a bed, she couldn't stop thinking about being with him in other ways. She wanted to talk to him, get to know him, laugh, tease, make memories. She wanted him to hold her close instead of stiffening every time she was near.

"Are you sure this is safe?" her mother asked as they crossed the stone courtyard leading to the stable. "Aren't there robbers and pirates in the desert?"

"Pirates are on the ocean," her father said gently. "However, we're going to have to deal with robbers."

Emma held in a sigh. She loved her parents very much but in the last couple of days they'd really started to get on her nerves. They weren't open to any new experiences and, despite the wonders of the palace, they kept talking about how much they wanted to go home. When she encouraged them to make plans they refused, telling her they wouldn't leave without her. The thought of two months in such close quarters made her teeth ache.

But that was a problem for another time. Right now she had to worry about the fact that Reyhan stood by the front of the stable, and upon seeing him she felt her heart rate quadruple while her thighs began to quiver.

"Good morning," Reyhan said as they approached.

He wore riding boots, dark slacks and a loose white shirt. Despite the short hair and freshly shaven face, Emma had the thought that he looked as dangerous as the pirates her mother feared.

But as appealing as she found him, he didn't seem to return her interest. He neither looked directly at her nor acknowledged her personally. He motioned to a large open vehicle—part roofless SUV, part topless van. There were three rows of seats.

"You'll be comfortable for our trip out to the oasis."

"Is it safe?" her mother asked. "Are there a lot of wild people and robbers on the loose?"

Emma winced. "Mom," she said quickly, "Bahania is a very civilized country."

Reyhan's expression didn't change. "The laws of the desert offer hospitality to all who enter. You will be welcomed by my people and treated as an honored guest." He motioned to the vehicle.

Emma's parents exchanged a glance before cautiously stepping inside. She hung back, wanting more than an impersonal trip with a man who was doing his best to become a stranger.

"I thought we'd be riding," she said.

He looked at her for the first time that morning. She felt the impact of his gaze all the way down to her already-curling toes.

"Do you know how?"

"I've had a few lessons." When she was twelve. "I'm a whiz on horses made of wood, but I can probably handle the real thing if he or she is gentle and doesn't think tossing me would be good for a chuckle."

Reyhan's dark eyes didn't flicker, not did his mouth even twitch. When exactly had he turned into a man of stone?

"Wait there," he said, and walked into the stable.

"Emma, what are you doing?" her mother asked fretfully.

"Reyhan and I are going to ride."

Both of her parents shrank back in their seats. "You can't."

"Sure I can. It will be fun."

Her father frowned. "When did you get so adventurous?"

She considered the question. "I can't give you an exact date," she admitted, knowing her change of heart had something to do with finding out nothing in her life was as she had first thought. Her parents weren't perfect. In fact they'd lied and kept the truth from her. Sure their actions had been in the name of keeping her safe, but she'd been an adult. The decisions hadn't been theirs to make. Not only that, but she'd been married for the past six years and hadn't had a clue. Information like that was bound to produce a change.

Reyhan returned, leading a beautiful white stallion. Emma might not know much about horses, but she'd heard rumors.

"Isn't he going to be too much for me to handle?" she asked, trying not to back up as Reyhan and the horse approached. Up close the animal seemed extremely large.

"He can have a temper, but he's very fond of the ladies."

The horse in question tossed his head, then seemed to give her the once-over. He looked large enough to pound her into the ground with just one hoof—the thought of which didn't exactly give her a warm fuzzy feeling inside.

"Great," she murmured. "A sexist horse. What's his name?"

For the first time in days, Reyhan smiled at her. "Prince."

"How appropriate."

She approached the powerful horse and tentatively stroked his nose. Prince stepped in close and rubbed his head against her arm, then bumped her side and exhaled.

"Is he flirting with me?" she asked, not wanting to know what the big animal would do if he lost his temper.

"Yes. He likes you. We'll ride out and take the Jeep back."

Reyhan murmured something to the horse, then moved to its side and made a step by lacing his fingers together. Emma remembered enough from her long-ago lessons to know she was expected to jump right up in that saddle. She sucked in a breath for courage and put her foot in his hands.

Not only was Prince's back about four hundred feet from the ground, the English saddle she settled in offered about as much protection as a handkerchief.

"There's nothing to hang on to," she said rather desperately as Reyhan handed her the reins.

"You'll be fine."

She would be maimed and possibly crippled, she thought, fighting fear. Reyhan disappeared into the stable, presumably to get his own horse.

"Emma, you can't ride that beast," her mother said. "It's not safe. Come down right now and sit with us."

The order gave her the impetus to stiffen her spine and smile brightly. "I'll be fine. We aren't going to go all that fast."

At least she hoped they wouldn't. It was a long way to the ground.

Reyhan returned with an even bigger gray stallion and mounted easily.

"The Jeep takes a longer route using the main road," he told her. "We'll cut across the desert and meet your parents at the oasis."

"Works for me," she said, thinking time alone with him might give them a chance to talk.

He waved off the driver and the Jeep pulled out. Reyhan gave her a few instructions, then watched her ride in slow circles. She found that her lessons from long ago came back to her and she quickly settled into the horse's rhythmic gate. After a few minutes, Reyhan led the way off the stable grounds and into the wild beauty of the open desert.

The morning was warm and brilliantly sunny. She was grateful for her hat and the sunscreen she'd slathered on her face. The hard-packed trail was easy to spot. She and Prince walked along behind Reyhan and his mount. When they went faster, Prince also picked up the pace. There were a couple of minutes of bone-jarring trotting before they settled into an easy canter. Reyhan pulled his horse to the side of the trail so they could ride next to each other.

The wind tugged strands of hair free from her braid. She tossed her head to get them out of her face and nearly slid off her horse. Reyhan shot out a hand and grabbed her arm. She managed to stay in the saddle, but only just. The slick leather seat suddenly felt smaller and more precarious.

"We will walk the rest of the way," Reyhan called as he tugged on his reins.

She slowed Prince, then glanced at the man next to her. "Sorry to be a bother."

"The fault is mine. You took to the riding so easily, I thought you were more experienced."

They walked side by side. Emma chose, then discarded several possible conversational openings. They all sounded forced and stupid, so she settled on the truth.

"I know you didn't want to do this today. Be with me and my parents, I mean. I appreciate you arranging everything and then coming along."

"It is important that you all enjoy your time in Bahania."

Before they left, she thought glumly.

"Seeing the desert will help you understand our ways," he said. "The desert is filled with tradition. For centuries nomads have wandered through the vastness of these lands. Thieves preyed on those using the silk road."

"Great. My mother was worried about being robbed."

He raised his eyebrows. "Those times are long past. Today those who live in the desert protect the oil fields to earn their living. A combination of the old ways and the new."

"Sounds like a good plan."

He shrugged. "There are those who do not wish to work. They want to take—much like the thieves of old."

She glanced around at the rolling dunes, the few clusters of scrubby plants. "Take what?"

"Money. They threaten our oil fields with disaster if we don't pay them off."

She caught her breath. "That's illegal, isn't it?"

"Yes. We know who these boys are. Most are second and third sons of nomadic chiefs. As they will not inherit, they are locked out of the family wealth. Instead of earning a living, they seek something more profitable and to their minds, easier. They play at being men."

"Are you going to have them arrested?"

He shook his head. "I have given my word to their fathers that I won't lock them up without cause. Mere threats are not considered cause, not out here. So we wait and watch. Sometimes angry young men grow up. Sometimes not."

"I don't understand," she admitted. "Why wouldn't their fathers want them to go to prison? What they're doing is wrong."

"To a man of the desert, there is no greater torture than to be locked away from the sun. I won't arrest anyone until he gives me a reason. This information does not make my head of security very happy."

"Hardly a surprise."

This was the longest conversation they'd had since they'd spent the night together. Emma wondered if Reyhan was thawing toward her or simply making the best of a bad situation.

"I'm sorry this is so difficult for you," she said. "Having me stay. Having my parents here. All of it."

"The time will pass."

Not exactly words to warm her heart. She wanted to remind him that a few days ago he'd wanted her with a passion that had thrilled them both. That he had kissed her and touched her. Remembering their time together made her stomach clench and her body burn.

"What if I just left?" she asked.

He continued to look straight ahead. "Nothing would change. When you returned, the ticking clock would continue. My father can be most stubborn."

She thought about how Reyhan avoided her as if she had some disease he didn't want to catch. How he barely spoke to her and never laughed anymore. The stubbornness seemed to be an inherited trait.

They arrived at the oasis about an hour later. Emma's parents were already there and rushed to greet their daughter. Reyhan watched them, wondering at their anxiousness. She had been with him and he would have died to keep her safe. Not that her parents had ever trusted him.

He dismounted and moved beside Emma's horse. Her mother glared at him as he helped Emma down. Even with her parents watching and disapproving, he noticed the warmth of her body and the way she leaned against him while she regained her footing.

"So I have a way to go before I'm an accomplished horsewoman," she said with a smile. "At least I survived."

He wanted to smile back at her and tell her that he would be happy to teach her to ride. He wanted to put his arm around her and draw her closer against him. He wanted to kiss her and touch her and be with her. Instead he stepped back and turned away.

"This oasis is not considered large. There are others deeper in the desert that cover several acres. But many families travel here because they can be close to the city while maintaining their old ways."

"Is it safe for us to wander around?" Emma asked. "Are there any things we shouldn't do? I don't want to offend anyone."

"You are an honored guest. You will be welcome." He looked at the small campsite set up around the pond of water. Children played with each other. The women talked together over the open fires, while the men tended the camels. Their arrival had been noticed, but his people would wait for him to make the first move.

"You have nothing to worry about," he said.

"Are you sure?"

He nodded, not surprised by her concern. One of the things he'd liked about her when they'd first met had been her soft heart. She cared about others—an unusual characteristic in the women he generally met.

Emma linked arms with her parents. "Isn't this fabulous?" she said happily. "Let's go introduce ourselves."

"They're strangers," her mother said. "We don't know if they speak English."

"Most do not," he confirmed.

"Then we'll have to fake it," Emma said, and pulled her parents toward the women.

He resisted the need to walk with her and claim her as his own by staying close. His presence was enough protection, he reminded himself. Even though she didn't need any.

He looked at the men hovering by the pen of camels. When he nodded, they approached, then bowed and offered greetings of respect. He recognized the oldest man, the chief of the small tribe, as someone who had ridden the desert with his father.

"Bihjan," he said, returning the bow. "I bring greetings from my father."

"I return those greetings and wish blessings on you and your family."

"And to yours."

The old man looked at Emma and her parents. "She is as beautiful as the sunrise."

Pride filled Reyhan. "My wife."

The old chief showed no surprised. "I see your blessings have already begun. You care for her."

Reyhan nodded rather than speak the truth—that *care* didn't come close. She was his life, his breath, and he wasn't sure he would survive without her.

"She will give you fine sons."

"If it is to be," he said simply, ignoring the tightness in his chest when he thought about children. He and Emma had made love without protection. He'd been so caught up in the moment, he'd never thought, never considered the consequences. If she was pregnant…

He cast the worry away. She couldn't be. If she were pregnant, she would stay forever, and being with her would destroy him. But to have a child with her…

He returned his attention to the chief. "You have been blessed with many sons," he said.

Bihjan nodded, his eyes dark with worry. "My

youngest son, Fadl, leads the renegades," he said quietly. "I know what they do, what threats they make."

"I have given my word," Reyhan reminded the old man. "If their threats remain empty, then I will do nothing. Perhaps in time, they will grow up enough to rejoin their people and become honorable men."

Bihjan sighed with relief. "I had heard it was so, but I wanted to ask for myself. I know these young men try your patience."

"My security chief's, as well. He believes they should be arrested and put in prison. I have explained that to be so confined is a form of death for men of the desert." He narrowed his gaze. "But be warned. My patience has limits. If any of the renegades acts in the smallest way, if their talk becomes action, my retribution will be swift and severe."

The old man nodded. "As it should be, Prince Reyhan. As it should be."

Emma loved everything about the oasis. The people were charming and at least two of the women understood a little English—at least enough for them to attempt to communicate. The children were beautiful and friendly and fun. She adored the dogs and the baby camels and the clever way the camp itself came together after being carted across miles of desert. Even her parents seemed to be having a reasonably good time, asking questions more than complaining. Maybe there was hope for them after all.

"They have invited us to dine with them," Reyhan said as he came up to stand next to her. "I have accepted."

Emma instantly glanced at the pen holding the camels and swallowed. "So, uh, what will be on the menu?"

Reyhan smiled. "Fear not. It's chicken."

"That's a relief. I don't think I could chow down on something I'd just petted and cooed over."

"I would not expect you to." He took her arm and pulled her away from everyone. "I told them you were my wife, without mentioning the pending divorce."

"Okay. That makes sense. The situation is complicated." She didn't know how to tell him she didn't mind him claiming her as his wife with no "but" tacked on.

"I wanted you to know," he said.

"Thank you."

They were called to dinner. Everyone sat around in a circle. Dishes were passed from person to person. Emma sampled spicy rice casseroles and tender chicken. There were flat breads and grilled vegetables. Two teenage boys played three-stringed musical instruments and a young girl with bells around her wrists and ankles danced for them.

"Can they afford to feed us like this?" Emma asked after a tray of honey-coated dates were offered. "I don't want them to starve or anything because they played generous host with us."

His dark gaze lingered on her face. "I appreciate your concern for my people. Do not worry. I have taken care of things."

She trusted that he had. Reyhan was a good man, a man she could admire. What would he say if he knew that she wanted these people to be her people, as well? That the more time she spent in Bahania, the more she liked the country and was confident she could have made a home here?

After the meal, several of the women rose and disappeared into one of the tents. A few of the men wandered off toward the camels. Emma started to rise, but Reyhan put a hand on her arm.

"There's more to come," he said.

"I'm pretty full."

"It's not food."

Sure enough, a young girl walked up and knelt in front of Emma. She held out her hand, offering a beautiful blue and red enameled necklace. Emma looked at it, then at him.

"I can't take that."

"You have to. You're their princess and they want to show respect." He leaned close and lowered his voice. "Don't worry. All that is expected is that you are enthusiastic and love everything. When we leave, the gifts stay behind."

"Good thing," she murmured as she noticed a teenage boy leading several camels toward her.

Still caught up in how Reyhan's warm breath had tickled her skin, she accepted the necklace, kissed the girl on both cheeks and thanked her warmly. Reyhan slid the necklace over her neck.

There were more pieces of jewelry offered, several bolts of amazing silk, four adult camels and one baby camel. The only gift she had trouble returning was a sweet puppy who licked her entire face and wiggled to get closer.

When she'd thanked everyone and carefully left all the smaller gifts on a blanket by the fire, she walked toward the SUV with Reyhan.

"They were wonderful people," she said. "Do the children go to school?"

He nodded. "They attend several months at a time, then return to their families. We are fortunate in that we can afford excellent teachers and modern schools that can meet the needs of children from the city and from the desert."

Emma thought about what Cleo had said—how she did charity work in her free time. Would that have been available to Emma, as well? Although she loved her job and knew she helped through one of life's greatest miracles, she was willing to admit to wanting to help on a grander scale.

Not likely, she told herself. Not when she was leaving and Reyhan was marrying someone else.

By the end of the week, Emma's parents had settled into life in Bahania. Emma was pleased to watch their attitudes slowly change from hostile mistrust of everything to pleasant acceptance. She would have loved to discuss the surprising transition with Reyhan but he continued to avoid her. So much for spending their days and nights together, she thought as she leaned close to the mirror and applied mascara to her lashes. They might physically be in the same palace, but they rarely spoke anymore. Reyhan worked impossible hours then disappeared into the guest room. The only time she saw him was at command dinners by the king.

At least tonight would be different. There was a large formal state occasion that was doubling as a welcome party for her parents. Reyhan had already informed her he was to be her escort. She would have been a lot more excited if he'd at least pretended to be happy about spending the evening with her. Instead he'd looked about as thrilled as a man facing the loss of both legs and an arm. She was determined to change his mind.

After finishing with her makeup, she pulled the hot rollers out of her hair, then fluffed the ends. After bending over at the waist, she sprayed her hair from underneath, then flipped her head to let the curls fall back into place.

"Not bad," she murmured as she finger combed a few wayward strands.

Next up was the bronze beaded evening gown. She slipped it on and pulled up the zipper, then stepped into her high-heeled sandals.

She studied her reflection and knew this was as good as it was going to get. If she couldn't dazzle Reyhan like this, it wasn't going to happen.

"Good luck," she whispered to her reflection, then walked out of the bathroom and into the sitting area.

Reyhan was already there. She nearly stumbled when she saw him in his well-tailored tux. His shoulders were broad and strong, his features lean and handsome. Her heart swelled with an affection she didn't want to name.

"You look beautiful," he told her.

"Thank you. You look great, too."

He held out a velvet-covered box, about ten inches square and only a couple of inches deep.

''For you.''

She hesitated before accepting the gift and opening it. When she saw the contents, her breath caught in amazement.

A yellow diamond necklace lay on a bed of white silk. The graduated diamonds had to be at least three carats each in front, and nearly a carat in back by the clasp. Two clusters of yellow diamonds formed earrings and there was a white and yellow diamond bracelet.

Emma reached for the necklace only to find she was shaking too much to pick it up.

''I can't,'' she told him. ''It's too much.''

''You are my wife,'' Reyhan said, taking the box from her and setting it on the table. He removed the necklace and placed it around her neck. ''Who would wear these if not you?''

''The next woman you marry,'' she said as he handed her the earrings. ''You'll want these things passed down to your children.''

As she spoke, she looked at him. Some emotion crossed his face but it was gone before she could read it. Awareness crackled between them and when he held out the bracelet to her, she wanted desperately to toss it aside and fling herself in his arms instead.

But she didn't. She let him fasten on the bracelet, then admired the fiery stones. She would wear these lovely things tonight but with the intent of leaving them behind. They were a part of his heritage and she had no right to claim them. If things had been different... But they weren't.

"Reyhan—" She touched his forearm, feeling the warmth of him and the tension of his muscles. "I want to mention something. About when we were together."

He didn't speak but a muscle twitched in his jaw. "There is nothing to say."

"Yes, there is. We didn't..." She cleared her throat. "When we made love..." She stopped and gathered her thoughts. "We didn't use any protection. I wasn't sure if you were worried about consequences. There aren't any. I wanted to reassure you that I wasn't pregnant."

"I see. You're sure?"

More than sure. Three days ago she'd gotten her period. "Positive."

He didn't say anything else as he led her to a large mirror in the dining room. He placed her in front of it and stood behind her with his hands on her shoulders.

"The jewels complete you," he said.

She looked at the elegant stones glittering at her ears and around her neck. They were lovely, but they didn't complete her. Only he could do that.

She wanted to know what he'd thought about the possibility of her being pregnant. Had he even considered it? Had he worried? Wondered? Had he hoped?

She had. Now that she knew for sure she wasn't pregnant she could admit that there had been times she'd thought it would be a good thing. That having a child together would be what they needed to connect. The truth or a schoolgirl fantasy? Now she would never know.

"Are you ready?" he asked, holding out his arm.

She nodded and slipped her hand into the crook of his elbow. They walked out of the suite together.

Emma had seen the formal ballroom on her tour with Reyhan but standing in the large empty space hadn't prepared her for the reality of seeing it filled with elegantly dressed people, sparkling lights and a full orchestra.

There were about five hundred guests, including several prime ministers and heads of state. A film crew working on an action movie in the desert had been invited, along with a former American president and a Nobel Prize winner.

Reyhan introduced Emma to many of the guests. She smiled, said little and reached for a second glass of champagne from a waiter circulating with a tray.

"Are you doing all right?" Reyhan asked quietly.

"Considering this is my first official function as a princess, I'm doing great. We'll ignore the butterflies in my stomach, my knocking knees and the nearly overwhelming urge to bolt for the gardens. I have to admit I'd feel a lot more comfortable with the king's cats."

Reyhan smiled. "You're charming and well-spoken. Everyone is impressed."

His compliment made her beam. Just then her parents walked up. They were actually smiling. Could this evening produce any more surprises?

"Kitten, you look beautiful," her father said. "Nearly as lovely as your mother." He kissed his wife's cheek.

Emma's mother dimpled. "Oh, George, you're just saying that." She leaned close to her daughter. "Isn't this party wonderful? We met that action star your father likes so much. Johnny Blaze. He was very pleasant, although his girlfriend looks thin enough to need Third World aid. And did you see the former president? He was very nice, too. Oh, and the king told us he's sending us on a cruise on his private yacht. We're going to explore the Mediterranean for a couple of weeks."

Emma nearly dropped her champagne glass. "You're going?"

"Of course. It's a once-in-a-lifetime opportunity. He said the boat's captain knows all the best places to take us."

Her father winked. "It will be like a second honeymoon."

Janice Kennedy actually giggled, then waved at Emma and Reyhan. "You two kids enjoy yourself. We have more famous people to meet."

Emma watched them walk off. "That was pretty amazing. I owe the king big-time. Not that I don't love my folks. I do. But they can be—"

"Oppressive?"

She smiled. "Absolutely. And a little judgmental. I hope they enjoy their cruise."

"I'm sure they will."

And she and Reyhan would be able to spend time together without her parents hanging around. The only trick would be getting him out of his office and paying attention to her. For that she would need a plan—and she would come up with one, just as soon as the champagne-induced fuzziness wore off.

The orchestra struck up another song, one that made her want to be in Reyhan's arms. She looked around and saw several of the guests dancing. They swayed to the music and laughed.

"You are more easy to read that usual," Reyhan said, taking her glass from her and setting it on a table in the corner. "Come. I will dance with you."

She was so pleased, she didn't bother to worry that he was doing her a favor. Not when he pulled her into his arms and held her close. If only the song could last forever, she thought happily.

Reyhan rubbed his hands against Emma's back and wished they were alone. Rather than dancing to music he wished to move with her in other ways. Perhaps it was the night, or how she looked or the invitation he saw in her eyes, but for some reason his resistance to her charms was weaker than ever.

He wanted her. More frightening than the desire was the truth that he wanted her in and out of his bed. He wanted to be with her, talk with her. He wanted to learn her secrets, discuss the future, name children and grow old with her. He wanted her to be his wife in every sense of the word.

He had the answer to his question about the baby. There wasn't one and he couldn't risk creating one with her. Yes, there was protection and it could be used, but that wasn't the point. He had escaped the possibility and he would be a fool to risk a pregnancy.

But he had always been a fool where Emma was concerned. From the first moment he'd met her that night on campus. She had smiled at him and he had been lost.

She swayed with him, sighing softly and snuggling close. She belonged, he thought. Whether laughing with his people in the desert or conversing with heads of state. She fit in. She made people feel at ease and never expected to be the center of attention. She was smart, kind and a woman of honor.

The fire always lurking below the surface flared to life and began to consume him. The need grew until he had no choice but to give in. He took her hand in his and pulled her toward a small alcove behind on of the decorated pillars.

"But the dance isn't over," Emma said. "Can't we finish the dance?"

Instead of answering, he drew her close and kissed her.

She melted into his embrace, parting her lips instantly and clinging to him. She stroked his tongue with her own and moaned softly. Her hands slipped under his jacket where she rubbed his back.

"Better than dancing," she whispered when he pulled back to kiss her jaw, then her neck. "I'll give up dancing for kissing you anytime."

He nibbled the sensitive skin below her ear and made her groan. She reached for his hands and brought them to her breasts.

As he cupped her full curves, he stared into her eyes and saw an answering passion there.

"Make love with me," she pleaded.

He knew how right it would feel. How good things would be between them. He knew she was wet to his hard, yielding and aroused. He knew he could claim her, mark her, make her his. And he knew the price he would pay if he did.

Without saying a word, he dropped his hands to his sides, turned and walked away. Emma's soft cry of pain made him pause, but only for a second. Then he resumed his stride and left the ballroom without looking back.

Chapter Eleven

Emma couldn't tell how much of the ache in her body came from her champagne hangover and how much came from humiliation. It wasn't just that Reyhan had left her alone at the party, it was that he'd kissed her and touched her, making her think he wanted her, and then he'd walked away. She felt both hurt and bruised, as if he'd been playing kick ball with her heart.

She curled up in the dining room chair and tried to work up some interest in the breakfast laid out there, but it wasn't happening. She'd taken a walk on the balcony encircling this level of the palace and that hadn't helped, either. Maybe she should shower and see if she could wash away the sense of having been a fool for a man who hadn't even noticed.

She stood and stretched. The good news is her parents were heading off to have a good time. The cruise was leaving that afternoon. As far as she could tell, they hadn't witnessed her humiliation, so she wasn't going to have to talk about it with them. But that didn't mean she wasn't going to stop thinking about it.

She headed for the bathroom. What had gone wrong? One second Reyhan had been kissing her as if he'd really enjoyed it. He'd been the one to pull her into the alcove, he'd been the one touching her. Except she'd brought his hands to her breasts. Had he disliked her being aggressive? Did *he* need to be in charge?

She didn't want to think that was true. He'd never been weird about having to ''be the man.'' Not that she had a whole lot of sexual experience with him or anyone. Had she freaked him out when she'd—

Emma had been so deep in thought she hadn't noticed the steam and heat in the bathroom. It was only as she came around the corner and saw Reyhan stepping out of the shower that she realized she wasn't alone.

He was wet and naked. Water dripped from his arms and legs, from his hair. Droplets ran down his cheeks. Her gaze met his and she found herself unable to turn away.

In less than two seconds, she went from hurt and hungover to hungry. She wanted to touch him all over and have him touch her back. She was aware of his arousal growing, thickening. As if he was getting as turned on as she was.

She licked her lips. "What are you doing here? You're usually gone long before I wake up."

"I went riding at sunrise and came back to shower."

He was now fully erect. The sight of him made her midsection clench. He obviously wanted her, so why was he just standing there?

He reached out his arm. For one brief heartbeat, she thought he was going to pull her close. Instead he grabbed a towel and turned his back on her.

"I'll be done in a few minutes."

It was a very polite invitation to leave.

Emma dropped her head, realized the sudden burning in her eyes came from unshed tears and fled to her bedroom. She closed the door behind herself and leaned against it.

Ten days ago she'd considered the king's insistence that she stay for another two months a stroke of good fortune. Now it was torture—a prison sentence that trapped her with a man who wanted nothing to do with her.

Reyhan read his e-mail without understanding what any of it said. Instead of words he saw Emma's hurt eyes and the tears that had filled them as she turned away from him and fled the bathroom. Two hours and three meetings later, he hadn't been able to erase the memory of her confusion and pain.

He'd caused her that pain. No matter how much he wanted to escape the truth, it remained. He'd never meant to hurt her and the need to make it up to her was strong.

He instantly thought of returning to their room and offering her what they both wanted. That would ease the throbbing inside of him and hopefully bring her pleasure. But he couldn't risk it for himself and he wouldn't make her promises he did not intend to keep.

Determined to lose himself in his work, he returned his attention to his e-mail. An hour or so later, his phone buzzed and his assistant announced that Will was on the phone.

"There's been a change in circumstances," his head of security said as soon as Reyhan came on the line.

Reyhan swore. "What?"

"I'm holding Fadl."

Fadl was the son of a prominent chief. "What happened?"

"He was caught stealing drilling equipment. Two other men were with him."

Reyhan frowned. "Did he say why he wanted it?"

"He's not talking. I have a few theories of my own. He could sell it on the black market and make a few bucks."

"That sounds like too much work for him and his friends."

"Agreed. He could also sabotage it somehow and then return it to inventory. When the replacement parts were put into service, we could have a pretty impressive disaster."

Reyhan shook his head. Was that possible? Had the boys decided to act on their threats? "We're going to have to inspect all parts in inventory and anything put into service in the past few months.''

''I've already got men on that. I'm also rounding up the rest of his buddies. They've scattered so it may take a while.''

''Keep on it. I'll be there in a couple of hours.''

''Good. Maybe Fadl will talk to you. I'm getting nowhere.''

''I'll see what I can do. As the prince, I can make certain threats to his family he wouldn't believe from you. I'll be there shortly.''

''We'll be waiting.''

Reyhan hung up the phone and considered his options. While he had been willing to keep his bargain with the chiefs up to a point, the rules had now changed. If Fadl was stealing—or worse, sabotaging—then he and his friends had to be stopped. Being young and sons of chiefs would not protect them anymore.

He called his assistant into his office and made arrangements for his meetings to be rescheduled. Once he'd reserved the helicopter and told the pilots where they were going, he walked to his father's offices. The guards there waved him inside, where he found the king on the phone.

''Reyhan,'' his father said cheerfully when he'd hung up. ''What brings you to me this fine morning?''

''Will has detained Fadl, Bihjan's son.'' He quickly recounted what his security chief had told him.

King Hassan didn't look happy. ''Have they moved from making threats to acting on them?''

''That's what I plan to find out. Will is going to

invite Fadl's friends to join him in custody. We'll send a team in to search their camp. If they've already sabotaged replacement parts we should find evidence. Regardless, all the equipment will be inspected.''

"Which means shutting down production for a few days.''

Reyhan had already done the calculations. ''We'll be back online at the end of the week.'' He shook his head. ''There is also the possibility this was Fadl's plan all along. To get caught in such a way that we would have to shut down. But I won't take the risk. All the wells will be inspected.''

"What are the international ramifications?''

"Minimal. We'll issue a statement saying we're running scheduled inspections, and production for the next month will be increased to make up the difference.''

The king raised his eyebrows. ''But the inspections aren't scheduled.''

"They are now.''

"Good point. When do you leave?''

"As soon as we're done here.''

"I'm sure Emma will enjoy the trip.''

Reyhan stared at his father. ''You can't be serious. I am not taking her with me.''

"Of course you are. You already have their leader in custody and will soon have the rest of his men. She won't be in any danger. If you're truly concerned about her standing out, have her put on native dress. I'm sure she'll look especially fetching.''

Reyhan glanced at the sleeping tabby on the sofa in the corner and thought about throwing the creature at his father. But he recognized the stubborn look in the king's eyes and knew he didn't have a choice. Take Emma. It was a ridiculous request, and he refused to acknowledge the sudden pleasure he felt.

He left his father and headed for his rooms. At least Fadl's activities had been more passive than violent. Reyhan wouldn't have to worry about Emma walking into the middle of a gunfight.

He steeled himself, vowing not to react when he saw her. She sat on the sofa, reading and looked up when he entered.

"I have to go into the desert," he said. "I'll be gone a day or two. The king has suggested you accompany me."

Her green eyes were wide and unreadable. She looked both hurt and broken. As if her spirit had received one too many mortal blows.

That was his doing, he acknowledged shamefully. He'd been the one to reject her over and over. He reached for the phone and pressed three buttons. As he waited for his call to be answered, he wondered if there was some way he could explain so that she would understand and see this wasn't about her. Not really. His actions were about himself. Then he admitted he doubted that information would be of much comfort to her.

He made his request, hung up and returned his attention to her.

She hadn't moved, except to close the book. "Are they for me?" she asked, referring to the traditional garments he had ordered.

"Yes. I'll need you to wear them while we're at

the camp. I don't expect any trouble, but regardless, they'll keep you safe.''

''You don't want me to go with you,'' she said flatly.

''What I want isn't important.''

''It is to me.''

He stood behind a club chair and rested his hands on the back. ''This is business. There has been an arrest. I'm confident everything will go smoothly but as I am not completely sure, I would prefer you not be there.''

''So this is only about keeping me safe?''

He nodded.

''I don't believe you. Wanting me to stay is about more than that.'' She rose and faced him. ''I want to speak to the king and tell him you find my presence intolerable. There's no reason for me to stay here and both of us to be tortured. I don't believe that's his purpose. Once he knows there is no hope for a rec-onciliation, then he'll agree to the divorce and you'll be free of me.''

As she spoke, she squared her shoulders and met his gaze with a confidence that impressed him. The frightened little girl she had been was completely gone and in her place was a self-sufficient woman.

She stood before him, offering him his freedom and all he wanted was to pull her close and claim her as his own forever. He longed for her with a need that defied description and still he would let her go.

''When we return,'' he told her, ''we will both talk to the king.''

Light faded from her eyes, as if the last flame of

her spirit had been extinguished. Reyhan wanted to move closer, to touch her and tell her his reasons were not what she thought, but he stayed where he was and dug his fingers into the back of the chair.

"I guess I should pack a few things," she said tonelessly. "What do I wear under the robes?"

"Whatever will be most comfortable. The days are hot, the nights cool. Jeans or slacks will give you freedom of movement."

She nodded and headed for her bedroom. He retreated to his quarters where he quickly collected a few belongings. By the time he returned to the living room, the traditional robes had been left on the sofa.

Emma didn't recognize the woman in the mirror, but she didn't know how much of that had to do with the yards of fabric that covered her from head to toe and how much had to do with her bleeding to death from the inside out.

Reyhan wanted her to leave.

She supposed she'd known there were problems and that he didn't want to sleep with her again, but that was a far cry from having him practically jump with joy at the thought of never seeing her again. She'd hoped to shock him with her suggestion that she speak with the king and ask to leave sooner. Instead he'd agreed with her plan. He was going to get everything he wanted and she would spend the rest of her life in love with a man who didn't want to be with her.

Emma didn't know exactly *when* she'd fallen in love with him, or if it had been with her, buried for the past six years. Did it matter? More important than the how or when was the reality of losing Reyhan for a second time.

He escorted her to a helicopter. Nervous excitement at flying in one for the first time eased some of her heartache. She strapped herself in and picked up the headset Reyhan pointed to. When the engine roared to life and the rotors began to move, she understood that the headset was the only way they would be able to communicate.

"We're going about a hundred miles into the desert," he said into his microphone. "To the western edge of the central oil fields."

She could see his lips moving and hear the sound coming through her speakers. The helicopter rose.

Emma clutched the armrests as the aircraft zoomed up and forward, moving dizzyingly fast. The sensation was very different from a plane, but not unpleasant. She watched the edge of the city disappear under them, then there was only the vast stretches of nothing.

"A young man was arrested today," Reyhan said. "He was stealing replacement parts for the oil rigs. We're not sure if he planned to sell them on the black market or sabotage them and put them back into inventory."

"Faulty parts could create an economic and ecological disaster."

Reyhan nodded approvingly at her grasp of the situation. "Exactly. His friends are being rounded up and will also be arrested. The man we caught, Fadl, has been unwilling to tell us what he's up to. I want to talk to him and see if I can convince him to co-operate.''

She remembered what Reyhan had said about the nomads' need to be free. ''Will he go to prison?''

''Probably. It depends on the seriousness of his crime. In this case, simply stealing would be a relief to everyone.''

''An odd reality.''

He smiled. ''How true.''

She turned away because she didn't want to smile back. She didn't want to feel that things were once again well between them. How could he act as if nothing was wrong?

She stared out the window and reminded herself that he had made it clear from the beginning that he *wanted* her out of his life. She'd been the one to forget that and try to change the rules. Was it his fault he hadn't agreed?

''There is a small camp of nomads by the oil station,'' he said. ''They are friendly and you will be safe in their company. Even so I will assign two men to stay with you. Just in case.''

''That's fine. Are there any cultural rules I should keep in mind?''

''No. Simply be yourself and they will adore you.''

As I do.

He didn't speak the words, but Emma heard them. They hung in the silence between them as loud as the engine. She looked at Reyhan, but he was staring out of his window and she couldn't see his expression.

A trick of her own imagination, she told herself.

Nothing more. Her feelings for him weren't going to change anything and she had to remember that.

They touched down about an hour later. Emma saw the low buildings clustered together and the oil rigs beyond. To the left, a dozen or so tents were pitched close to the bubbling oasis. Reyhan had told her the pool was fed by an underground spring.

He climbed out of the helicopter first, then held out his hand to assist her. She took it and instantly felt the warmth of his fingers. Weakness invaded her, a weakness she had to learn to control and eventually conquer.

In time, she promised herself. She would heal in time.

Reyhan entered the interrogation room and stared at the young man sitting there. Fadl was all of eighteen, slightly built and sullen looking. The youngest son of a powerful chief. While he would not have inherited all his father's wealth, he could have made a good life for himself with the tribe. Instead, he'd chosen to take what he wanted.

"You have crossed me," he told the young man. "You knew that your father didn't want you harmed or arrested. He thought you would come to see the error of your ways. But I am not a foolish old man who still indulges a spoiled child. I am Prince Reyhan of Bahania and now we will play by *my* rules."

Fear flickered in Fadl's eyes. "That's a load of bull. You can't hurt me. You promised my father."

Reyhan allowed himself a small smile. "I agreed to let you run around and play at being a man until you broke the law. Which you did by stealing parts. Now the deal doesn't exist and you are mine."

The young man squirmed in his seat. "I don't believe you."

"Good. I will enjoy putting you in prison. Because of you, the oil rigs must be checked for sabotaged parts. That will cost my country hundreds of thousands of dollars. As I know you have no funds of your own to compensate me, I will take what I can out of your hide."

Fadl visibly paled. "How did you know that's what we were going to do?"

Reyhan kept his expression impassive. He'd guessed correctly. Now he simply had to get the details from the boy and let Will deal with damage control.

"What made you think you could succeed?" Reyhan asked. "You know nothing of the oil equipment. You certainly haven't worked the rigs."

Fadl shifted in his seat. "I don't want to go to prison."

"You don't have a choice. The question on the table is for how long. Please me and I will make sure your time there is almost pleasant. Annoy me and I will find a particularly uncomfortable place for you to call home."

There were several seconds of silence. In the end, fear won.

"It wasn't us," Fadl admitted. "Not really. A bunch of us were at a bar in El Bahar and we were trying to come up with a plan. This guy approached us. He said he'd been listening and that we were amateurs. If we wanted to make some big money, we needed to hire professionals. So we did.''

Reyhan's blood ran cold. He crossed to the door, pulled it open and yelled for Will to join them.

Fadl told them everything. The name of the man whom they'd hired, how many associates he'd brought into Bahania and how much Fadl and his gang were to pay them.

''We haven't put back any bad parts,'' Fadl said frantically. ''They're all in our camp. You have to believe me, Prince Reyhan. I swear. We were just after the money and this seemed like an easy way to get it.''

Reyhan stared at him with loathing. ''See if you feel that way after your stay in prison.''

Emma wandered around the oasis. Her bodyguards kept far enough away that she was able to forget about them. As she'd seen before on her outing with her parents, there were children playing and filling the afternoon with the sound of laughter. Several small dogs tumbled over each other in a game only they could understand. Women clustered together sewing and cooking and sending glances her way.

A little girl of about seven or eight ran up to her and offered a plate of dates. Emma smiled her acceptance and bit into one. Soon another little girl joined them, then another and another.

''I can't eat all these,'' Emma said with a grin as she touched the closest girl's smooth dark hair. ''But thank you for offering.''

A little boy tugged on her sleeve. She bent down

to his level and he pulled on her head covering. She reached up and slipped it down to her shoulders. All the children gasped at the sight of her red hair.

"I know. Not the usual thing," she said happily.

A girl reached out to touch it, then shrank away. Emma laughed.

"It's all right. It doesn't burn." She stroked her hair herself, then took the girl's hand in her own and brought it to the side of her head. The child touched her lightly, giggled and touched her again. The other children crowded close.

"My, my, my. Aren't you a pretty lady?"

At the sound of the male voice, the children scattered. Emma stood and turned, only to come face-to-face with two tall, armed strangers. Her bodyguards were nowhere to be seen.

"You're American," she said, trying not to betray her nervousness.

The man closest to her grinned. He had close-cropped blond hair and a tattoo of a snake on his forearm.

"Good guess," he said and stepped behind her. Before she could make a move, he had grabbed her and pulled her close, then pressed a knife to her neck. "And you're our prisoner."

"What the hell were you thinking?" Will demanded as he paced in front of Fadl. "You hired a man you met in a *bar*. Didn't it occur to you that he wasn't just a military consultant? Didn't you think you were getting in over your head?"

Fadl looked miserable, young and scared. "He said if we didn't do what he wanted, he'd kill us."

Reyhan stared at the boy. "You *wanted* to get caught," he breathed. "You need our help to get out of this mess."

Fadl nodded frantically. "Prince Reyhan, please. They're out of control. You have to help me. Help all of us. We're sorry. We didn't mean for any of this to happen."

"Of course you did. But now you've got a tiger by the tail and you don't know how to keep it from eating you." He looked at Will. "This is your area of expertise."

"I'm on it," his security chief told him. "I'll call in a team from El Bahar and—" he glanced at Fadl "—elsewhere."

Reyhan knew Will meant the City of Thieves, a secret city in the middle of the desert on the border with El Bahar and Bahania.

"I know the head of security there," Will continued. "Rafe Stryker and I have worked together before."

"Good."

Will started to leave, but before he reached the door, a man burst into the room. He ran to Reyhan.

"She was taken by two Americans. They shot one of the men guarding her and knocked out the other. They have Princess Emma."

Reyhan went very still and very cold. He looked at Fadl. "If she is harmed in any way, the desert will run red with your blood."

Chapter Twelve

"So how many millions are you worth, sweetheart?" the man with the tattoo asked as he pushed Emma into the back of a truck.

The gag in her mouth made it impossible to speak, so she could only glare her rage.

"I didn't know Prince Reyhan was married or I would have planned this better," the man said with a grin. "Guess I just got lucky today. Don't worry. No one wants to hurt you. I thought those unhappy kids would be our ticket to the easy life, but they turned out to be all talk. When it came right down to doing the dirty work, they got scared. Said they didn't want to blow up any oil wells. So I figured I'd wasted my time. Then you came along."

Emma wanted to shriek her outrage. She couldn't

believe this was happening. If she could just get her hands loose she would claw her kidnapper's eyes out.

Her anger pleased her. It meant she wasn't going to be immobilized by fear. She had to stay strong so that when the time came she could escape.

The man fingered a strand of her hair. "I'm guessing your old man is going to pay through the nose to get you back in his bed."

A knife flashed. Emma jumped back but not before her capture sliced off a lock of her hair.

"Just so he knows I'm not bluffing," the man said, and slammed the door.

She found herself alone and in darkness. The hum of a motor and cool air blowing over her told her there was an air-conditioning unit. At least she wouldn't die of heat exhaustion.

Don't give in to the fear, she told herself. She had to stay strong. She had to be prepared. The men who had taken her weren't going to kill her. She was too valuable for that. They wanted money, and lots of it.

Feeling her way along the inside of the compartment, she found a bench seat and lowered herself onto it. Her hands were tied behind her. Ropes cut into her wrists and as she struggled to loosen them, her shoulders began to ache.

How long would it all take? She knew that however much Reyhan might want her gone, he wouldn't ever just leave her like this. She knew he would rescue her. But when? And how could she hang on until then?

Fadl shrank back in his chair. He looked far younger than his eighteen years. "I swear I didn't know," he said as tears filled his eyes.

Reyhan didn't care. "You are responsible. I should kill you now."

Will grabbed his arm. "Killing him won't help. We have a situation."

He glared at his security chief. "They have taken my wife."

"I know. We'll get her back."

Reyhan felt himself consumed by the fires of rage. He wanted to destroy with his bare hands. He wanted, at his feet, the broken and bleeding body of the man who had dared to take Emma, and then he wanted the opportunity to kill him a second time.

Fear lurked inside him, as well. Fear for her and what she must be feeling. Fear that she wouldn't believe he would move the rotation of the earth itself to get her back. He'd been so cold, had rejected her so many times. His efforts to convince her he didn't care had been too successful by far. What if she thought he wouldn't be bothered?

He clenched his hands into fists and turned to Will. "Find out how much they want. This is all about money." Will nodded and left.

Reyhan glared at Fadl. "Your attempts to play at danger have cost me something precious. You will pay, as will your entire family. The cost will bleed down through a hundred generations of your people."

Fadl hung his head. "I'm sorry," he whispered through his tears.

Reyhan walked out of the room. He needed to move, to act, to do something. Instead he could only wait for information. In the main security center, a dozen men worked phones and computers. His security chief walked over to him.

"Reinforcements will be here within the hour," Will said. "Troops are coming in from El Bahar and the City of Thieves. I've got my best computer guy working on a special kind of Trojan horse. Basically it allows the ransom to show up in the offshore account, but it's only good for ninety minutes. Then poof, the money isn't there anymore."

"That doesn't give us much time to get Emma back," Reyhan said, knowing he would gladly pay any price for her safe return.

"We set up the exchange so that we're face-to-face when it happens. We see Emma, we send the money transfer. They get notification of the deposit and they release her. It should only take about five minutes. That gives us the rest of the time to get the hell away."

"Do it," he said.

Will nodded. "Just as soon as they tell us how much. We should—"

A young man in uniform came running up. "Sir, we've heard. Sixty million in euros. I have the account number."

Will looked at Reyhan who nodded. "Agree to it."

The young man swallowed. "There's something else, sir." He glanced from Will to Reyhan and back. "A storm. It didn't look like much an hour ago, but now…" His voice trailed off.

Reyhan's chest tightened. "Sandstorm?"

The officer nodded. "It looks bad."

Reyhan stared at Will. "The helicopters won't be able to fly."

Which meant the reinforcements wouldn't arrive anytime soon and Reyhan couldn't fly Emma to safety.

"We could stall them," the young man said. "Explain that it takes time to raise that kind of money and—"

"No!" Reyhan's gaze narrowed. "My wife is not to stay with them one second more than necessary. Do you understand?"

"Yes, sir. Of course." He scurried away.

Will shook his head. "It's more risky without the backup but we can still make it happen."

"We have no choice. If necessary, I will fight them all myself."

The tattooed-snake guy who turned out to be called Billy pulled Emma out of the truck.

"Looks like this is your lucky day, too, sweetheart," he said as he helped her to the ground. "Your old man is going to pay up. Sixty million euros. Not bad for an afternoon's work."

She was stunned. Sixty million euros? That was close to sixty million dollars. An insane amount of money. She couldn't imagine there was that much wealth in the whole world. Reyhan couldn't pay that. Just the thought of it made her sick to her stomach.

"You look shocked," Billy said. "Don't be. These prince guys really have a thing about other men hanging around their women. Of course I thought he'd try to negotiate me down a little, but he didn't. I'm not going to complain. That's twenty million for each of us.''

She glanced around the camp. The sky had darkened and the air seemed thick, but she could still make out nearly two dozen men. She looked at Billy.

He nodded. "I know what you're thinking. There's more than three of us here. But see, these aren't my guys. They're those kids who hired us. The ones who chickened out. So I say screw 'em. Me and my boys will be long gone with the money while these stupid kids take the fall. Good plan, huh?''

She nodded and wondered how she could get the information to Reyhan.

"Hold on," Billy said, and tugged at her gag. When it was removed, she sucked in a breath of air.

"Better?" he asked.

She nodded, her mouth too dry for her to speak.

He glanced at the sky. "There's a storm coming. Good for us, bad for them. They would have called in for help, but it ain't coming in the middle of a sandstorm. Come on, Princess. Your ride is this way.''

Emma followed the man. As she walked, she tried to figure out how long she'd been held in the truck. She would guess two or three hours at most. With clouds rolling in and covering the sun, there was no way for her to judge time that way. The air was so thick with sand that it was difficult to breathe.

Should she try to escape? If Reyhan had made a deal, maybe it would be better to go along with the plan. But she wanted him to know that the young men they had captured had nothing to do with the trouble.

* * *

"Be prepared," Reyhan told Will. "If things go badly and we can't get away in time, there could be a fight."

"Agreed." Will patted the gun at his side. "My men are ready."

Reyhan was also armed and determined. He'd given firm instructions that no one was to do anything until Emma was back in his arms. Once she was safe, their side would walk away.

"Is your team in place?" he asked Will.

The other man nodded. "They'll get behind the trucks and put on the tracking devices. Then when the storm lifts, we'll send in an armed contingent to take them." He grinned. "They won't know what hit them."

"Good."

Reyhan's first instinct was to punish the men immediately, but he had to think about Emma. Getting her to safety was his primary concern. The bastards who had taken her would be brought to justice. He would not rest until it was so.

He checked his watch, then stepped into the open Jeep. The vehicle offered little protection against the growing storm.

"It's time," he said against the wind.

Will started the engine and they drove into the desert.

Emma couldn't see anything. The sand was thick and hot and her face felt as if it were being scraped by sandpaper. She squinted against the windshield.

"How do you know where you're going?" she asked Billy.

He tapped the compass on the dashboard. "I'll find the rendezvous. Don't you worry, Princess."

She wasn't worried. Not for herself. Did Billy and his men have any idea about the danger they were in? Reyhan wasn't simply going to pay them, and if Billy thought he was, the man was a fool.

His two companions were in the truck behind them and the young nomad-rebels farther back.

"When will you three head out?" she asked casually, wishing he would untie her wrists. Her shoulders ached and her skin was raw.

"Don't even think you can bat your eyes at me and get me to spill my plans, Princess. You're pretty, but I'm not going to fall for it."

She shrugged as if it didn't matter, then stared out of the windshield.

Visibility had dropped to a few hundred yards. The road was covered with blowing sand and debris. She squinted as she thought she saw an outcrop of rocks in the distance.

"Here's the place," Billy said, stopping the truck. He took the keys and tucked them into his shirt pocket. "I'm going to leave you here, Princess. Tell me you're not stupid enough to try and escape into this mess."

"I'll stay here," she promised, knowing she would. Running now would be idiotic and suicidal.

Billy disappeared into the storm. Emma waited, trying to be patient, knowing Reyhan was close and wanting to run to him. But she couldn't be a distraction. He would have a plan and she didn't want to get in the way of that.

After what felt like a lifetime, but was probably only ten or fifteen minutes later, Billy opened the truck door.

"Show time," he said, and pulled out a knife.

He slit the ropes holding her wrists together. When she tried to move her arms, pain shot through her. She forced herself to ignore it and flex her arms until she could move them freely.

She saw Billy's two companions just behind him. They were equally scary with their close-cropped hair and multiple weapons.

"Climb on down," Billy said, motioning for her to step out of the truck.

When she stepped onto the ground she realized her escorts were the least of her problems. Sand attacked her like a giant angry beast. She couldn't see, couldn't breathe, could barely move. Grateful for the voluminous material covering her body, she pulled up her head covering and tugged the edges so she could protect her nose and mouth. Billy grabbed her arm and led her deeper into the storm. When they stopped, she looked up and saw Reyhan.

"I'm here," she called, trying to jerk free of Billy's hold.

The mercenary didn't let go. "Transfer the money," he yelled, then jerked his head toward his buddies. "Check the download."

The men pulled out small handheld devices. Emma strained to break free, never taking her eyes from Reyhan. He wore protective glasses and a heavy cloak, but she would swear he was staring right at her. She could almost hear his voice, willing her to be strong.

"Here it comes," Billy's friend yelled.

"What have you done?"

The fierce question came from somewhere on the left. Billy turned toward the man racing toward them.

"Shut up, kid. Stay out of this."

"No! You have kidnapped the wife of Prince Reyhan and now you ransom her?"

"Welcome to the games the big boys play. You and your friends were too much like girls to go through with your plans, so I had to pick up a little expense money elsewhere." Suddenly Billy was holding a gun in his other hand. "Stay out of this kid, or die. It's your choice."

Emma was so stunned, she nearly stumbled. "Don't hurt him," she demanded, pulling at her arm and suddenly jerking free.

Billy spun toward her. "Don't screw this up, sweetheart. I'll take you out if I have to."

"Emma."

She heard Reyhan's voice over the storm, over her fear and over the rapid pounding of her heart.

"Let her go," the first man insisted. He charged Billy.

Emma read the mercenary's intent before he ever acted. Even as he raised the gun, she flung herself at his arm, shoving him down. The gun went off.

The sound of the gunshot cut through the roar of the storm. Suddenly men where everywhere and bullets filled the air. Emma didn't know where to run or hide, nor did it matter. All she could think was that she had to get to Reyhan. Then something large and heavy crashed into her and she was trapped on the ground.

Panic flared. She couldn't breathe. She struggled until a familiar voice spoke into her ear.

"Be still. You are safe."

Reyhan. Fierce gladness swept through her and she wanted to roll over so she could cling to him.

More bullets cut through the storm. There were cries of pain, curses and the howl of the wind. Suddenly Reyhan was off her and pulling her to her feet. They were running toward the truck.

"Billy has the keys," she yelled to Reyhan. "In his pocket."

Reyhan didn't answer. Instead he circled around to the passenger side and shoved her inside.

"Stay down," he ordered. "Under the dash."

Then he was gone.

Emma huddled on the floorboards and prayed as she had never prayed in her life. That Reyhan would be safe. That no one else would be hurt. That they would all get out of this alive.

Time ticked by. Hours? Minutes? She wasn't sure. At last there was only the sound of the storm and she risked looking out the passenger window.

The three mercenaries were captured, sitting on the ground, their arms and legs bound. Several of the injured were being treated by men she thought must work for Reyhan. Relief coursed through her, making her weak and nauseated. They had survived.

After a time, Reyhan returned to the truck. "Are

you all right?'' he asked as he climbed in beside her and put a key in the ignition.

"I'm fine. Is there…'' She glanced out the window. "Are there a lot of injuries? My bodyguards?''

"A few. One of the mercenaries took a bullet to the arm. A couple of the rebels were shot, as were three of Will's men. None are fatal.''

"Good.'' She swallowed. "Was anyone killed?''

"One of the rebels. I knew him and his father. He was just seventeen.'' Reyhan looked weary and distressed.

Emma's stomach lurched. "Oh, God. It was my fault.''

"No.'' He turned on her. "Not your fault. These boys who wanted to play at being dangerous men brought this upon themselves. No one took them seriously, not even me. I knew their game and thought they would outgrow it. We were all wrong.''

He started the truck. "It's time to get you to safety.''

She was still stunned by the news that there had been a death. "I'm a nurse. I could help.''

"They'll be fine. Will's men are all trained in combat first-aid. He's very thorough. That's why I hired him.''

He started driving. She stared out the windshield and tried to come to terms with all that had happened in the past few hours.

"I'm sorry I was captured,'' she said. "I wasn't trying to make trouble.''

"The fault is mine. I shouldn't have allowed you to come here. I should have ignored my father.''

"Hard to do when he's the king."

Reyhan clutched the steering wheel more tightly. "He presumes too much and plays games with us all. This one could have cost you your life. I will never forgive him for that."

The force of his words stunned her. "Reyhàn, he didn't know. None of us knew."

"Agreed. But it was a possibility."

He was acting as if he cared. This from the man who couldn't wait to divorce her. Thoughts swirled in her head. She felt exhausted.

He read her mind. "Close your eyes," he told her. "Rest."

"No. I want to stay awake and keep you company on the drive." The storm still swirled around them and made visibility nearly impossible.

"I know my way."

She supposed he would. This was his land, his desert. She leaned against the side of door and let her eyes drift closed. Maybe she would relax for a couple of minutes. What could it hurt?

Emma drifted off to sleep. She didn't know how long she'd been out, but she was awakened by a horrible crashing as the truck roared into what looked like the side of a mountain.

For a second, she was disoriented. Not sure where she was or why, she frantically glanced around. When she saw Reyhan slumped over the steering wheel, her memory returned and with it, panic.

Had they run off the road? Why had he driven into the rocks? She unfastened her seat belt and scrambled across the bench seat, then eased Reyhan into a sitting position.

His face was unscathed. She checked for bumps and bruises, but there weren't any. He hadn't hit his head.

"Reyhan," she called frantically. "Can you hear me?"

He didn't answer.

Why was he unconscious? She began to check for other injuries. First his shoulders, then his arms. She slid her hand down his side and drew them back when she felt wetness. Blood covered her right hand.

"No!" she whispered, horrified and afraid. The thick stickiness told her he'd been bleeding for some time. Reality crashed in on her.

"You were shot," she breathed. "Oh, God. It can't be." Hadn't he known?

She glanced around frantically. She had to get him somewhere that she could examine him. Maybe the back of the truck. But without a first-aid kit, what could she do? She didn't even know where they were.

He stirred and groaned.

"Reyhan? Can you hear me? You've been shot."

He opened his eyes. "It's nothing."

"You're bleeding and you passed out."

He blinked at her, then stared out the front of the truck. "We're at the caves," he said.

"At them? We're practically in them." She looked at the crumpled front of the truck. "I'm not sure it's going to still run. Are we close to the security camp?"

He shook his head, then groaned. "We're at the

Desert Palace. My aunt's house. Through the caves. We need to go through the caves.''

Emma wasn't sure if he was delirious or not. But if there was a house nearby, maybe she could get some help.

She stepped out onto the ground. The storm had lessened to the point where she could see the landscape around them. They were in some kind of small canyon with the front of the truck mashed up against a sheer rock wall. To the right was an opening to a cave.

She turned in a slow circle and saw nothing. Not a road, not a building, not a hint of life. They were truly alone.

The fear returned and with it a conviction that she wouldn't let Reyhan die. She couldn't. He might not care about her, but she loved him.

She crossed into the mouth of the cave. The opening was huge with the ceiling soaring up what looked like two stories. There was a small chest to the right of the opening and she crossed to it.

She opened it and inside she found flashlights, batteries, water, food and a first-aid kit. When she turned back to the truck, she screamed. Reyhan leaned against the entrance. He was pale, shaking and bleeding.

"What are you doing?" she demanded as she raced back to him. "Stay still. You can't lose any more blood."

"It's about two miles that way," he said, pointing into the cave. "You'll have to pull the truck into the cave, then help me walk the rest of the way."

''You're not walking two miles anytime soon,'' she told him. ''We'll camp right here until help arrives.''

''Not likely soon, and there aren't enough supplies,'' he said, and winced.

She glanced at the food and water provided and knew he was right. The trunk provided emergency rations, not enough to live on.

''One thing at a time,'' she told him. ''I have to get you bandaged up. Then we'll talk about moving you.''

''We have to make the trip before dark,'' he said. ''There's not much time.''

Chapter Thirteen

Aware of the passage of time, Emma worked quickly. She pulled all the supplies out of the trunk and was relieved to find a blanket folded in the bottom. Once she had everything gathered, she helped Reyhan into a seated position.

His robes came off easily. Once she'd tossed them aside she could see the bloodstained shirt clinging to his torso. He barely hissed as she took off the drenched cotton, even when it pulled in places. When she was done, she examined the wound.

The bullet had gone through him. She had no way of knowing if anything vital had been damaged nor could she have fixed anything if it had.

Her emergency training came back to her and she worked quickly, grateful for her stint in the emergency room back home. Less than twenty minutes later she'd nearly stopped the bleeding, which meant she could finish bandaging the wound.

She was shaken, scared and ready for someone to rescue them, but she had a feeling they were on their own until she could figure out a way to call for help.

She crouched in front of Reyhan and smooth back his sweat-soaked hair. "I'm done," she whispered. "It shouldn't hurt so badly now."

"I'm fine."

She doubted that, but while the first-aid kit had plenty of bandages and antiseptic, there hadn't been any painkillers.

"Is there a cell phone I can use?" she asked. "Can I call for help?"

"In the Desert Palace," he said between clenched teeth. He sucked in a breath and rolled to his knees, then started to stand.

She clutched his arm. "You can't. We'll stay here."

"No. We go now. There's little time."

She glanced outside and figured they had about two hours left of daylight. Depending on how fast they could move, they had a chance of getting to the palace by dark. But it wasn't a sure thing.

"We should wait and go in the morning."

He looked at her. "You don't want to face what roams the desert at night."

Good point.

She collected their supplies and put them in the blanket, then knotted the ends together so she could wear it like a sling. She had them each drink some water, then she got Reyhan to his feet and leaned him against the wall. Finally she went out to the truck.

Surprisingly it started. She maneuvered it into the cave where it sputtered and died before she had a chance to turn off the ignition. So much for the backup plan of trying to find the camp via the truck.

She took one of the flashlights and handed the other to Reyhan. Then standing on his injured side, she took as much of his weight as she could.

It was slow going. She didn't want to think how much his side must hurt him or how weak and out of it he must feel from the blood loss. But he didn't complain, didn't slow down. He moved steady, at a pace that stunned her, turning left, then right, going deeper and deeper into the mountain, following directions only he could recognize.

There were hundreds of places to get lost, she thought nervously as they came to yet another fork in the path. Reyhan went to the left, passed three other trails, before picking the fourth.

Despite the distance they'd traveled, Emma knew they weren't going deeper underground because there were bits of light filtering through the rocks above. Although as time passed, the light seemed to get more and more dim.

"We're nearly there," he said, his voice low and raspy.

She stopped and urged him to lean against the wall. "Have some water," she said. "You're dehydrated."

He took the water and drank. His willingness to listen to her told her just how badly he'd been hurt.

They started walking again.

After about twenty minutes, Reyhan spoke. "There's a satellite phone in the office," he said. "Find it tonight and put it out in the courtyard tomorrow. There's a solar cell. It will take twelve hours to charge."

Twelve hours? That meant they couldn't call for help until tomorrow night. What if Reyhan was bleeding to death on the inside? What if the bullet had pierced his intestines or his spleen or…?

The path blurred and she realized she was crying. Blinking away the tears, she did her best to ignore the panic filling her and think about what was important. They'd survived this long. She could manage emergency first aid. Any crisis could be dealt with at the time. They would survive—she would make sure of it. She hadn't come this far and realized she loved him only to lose him now.

Nearly a half hour later, she realized the sun was definitely setting. Soon it would be completely dark except for the light from their flashlights. Her body ached from Reyhan leaning on her. She was tired, hungry and thirsty. If she felt this bad, he must feel a hundred times worse.

She was about to ask how much farther when he stopped and pointed. "There."

Emma peered into the murky darkness and saw what looked like a solid stone wall.

"It's a dead end," she said, fighting both panic and resignation. They weren't going to make it.

He glanced at her and raised his eyebrows.

"Do not believe everything you see. Go stand in front of the wall."

She made sure he was leaning against the rocks before shrugging off his arm and approaching the wall. She pressed her hand against the stones.

"Cold and solid."

"The bricks are a grid," he said. "Count across from left to right and down from top to bottom. Three over and five down. Push."

She blinked in the darkness, then did as he requested. The stone moved. Her heart nearly leapt out of her chest.

"It's working."

"Of course it is," he said, and gave her the next instruction.

So they went for a total of eight stones. On the last one, there was an audible click, then the stone wall swung in like a well-oiled door. The ground changed from uneven rock to polished stone and slowly sloped up.

"We are here," he said, and walked into the palace.

Emma followed him. Reyhan kept his balance by pressing one hand against the wall and holding his flashlight with the other. At the top of the ramp, they entered what appeared to be a basement or cellar. He turned a lever and the stone door swung shut.

"There is a short flight of stairs," he said. "On the main floor are several bedrooms, the kitchen and the office. You'll find the satellite phone in there."

He crossed the open area and headed for a flight of stairs at the far end. Emma was surprised that he barely limped. It was as if being in the Desert Palace gave him strength.

"Is there food and water?" she asked.

"Yes. No fresh food, but staples. And fresh water is always available. There's an underground spring."

He climbed the stairs, slowly only slightly toward the top. She saw blood seeping through his bandage and winced. "You need to lie down," she told him.

"Soon."

At the top of the stairs was another door. This one had a knob. He turned it and they stepped into a beautifully tiled hallway. The air was cool but fresh and there were still hints of sunlight coming in through large windows.

"There are battery-operated lanterns," he said. "Several in each room."

He moved down the hallway, pausing only to point out the direction to the kitchen, the placement of the office and where the wing of bedrooms began.

He entered the first one, made his way to the bed, sat down and passed out before he could put his head on the pillow.

Fear returned but by now Emma was familiar with the knot in her stomach and the tightness in her chest. She ignored it and went to work.

After setting down the supplies she carried, she found the battery-powered lantern in the room and clicked it on. Then she made sure Reyhan was comfortable on the bed and checked his wound.

The seepage from before had stopped, which was a relief. So far there was no red, swollen flesh to indicate infection. Was it possible they'd gotten off relatively easily?

Confident he was all right for the moment, she took

one of the flashlights and did a quick search of the main floor of the large house.

There were over a dozen rooms on this level and at least three staircases. The kitchen was huge and well stocked. Cold water gushed from the faucet. She found a propane-heated stove and oven, along with an empty refrigerator that probably needed a generator in order to run.

In the book-lined office, she found a case on the big desk that looked somewhat like a phone. She made a mental note to stick that outside sometime tonight so that it could start charging in the morning.

None of the four downstairs bathrooms offered a first-aid kit, so she returned to the kitchen and went into the pantry. Sure enough, on the bottom shelf was an assortment of medical supplies to supplement what had been in the first-aid kit in the case.

She collected what she needed and returned to Reyhan's room.

He hadn't moved. She checked his temperature, which was normal, then changed the bandage and decided to wait on everything else. If he regained consciousness, she would see if he could drink water and eat. If he didn't…she would face that problem later.

She returned to the kitchen where she dumped the old bandages and opened a can of soup. She ate it cold, too tired to bother with trying to heat it. After swallowing the contents and three full glasses of water, she made use of one of the luxury bathrooms, then returned to Reyhan's room.

He was still cool to the touch and there wasn't any more bleeding. She had no way to tell about internal injuries, but she was hopeful that he'd been very lucky and that the bullet had missed everything.

Weary behind words, she curled up next to him on the bed and closed her eyes. Just for a few minutes, she told herself. She still had to get the phone outside and figure out what she was going to feed him when he woke....

Someone stroked her hair. Emma felt the light touch even in her sleep and smiled. She was warm all over and rested and in just a second she would open her eyes and see—

Consciousness returned and with it the memories of what had happened the previous day. She sat up and realized it was morning and Reyhan was awake.

"Good morning," he said.

She stared at him, at his bare chest and the clarity in his eyes. His color was good. Except for the white bandage at his waist, she wouldn't have known he'd ever been injured.

"How are you feeling?" she asked.

"Good. A little sore, but otherwise fine. I am hungry and thirsty."

"Positive signs." She touched his forehead. "No fever?"

"Not that I can feel."

Suddenly aware that she was pressed against him and that they were on a bed, she shifted toward the edge then stood.

"Let me check your bandage. If there's no sign of infection, we can all breathe a little easier."

She removed the dressing. The wound was clean, the surrounding skin pale.

"It's already healing," she told him.

"Good. Then we can eat."

He swung his legs to the floor and stood. She hovered by his side, but he seemed fine. Strong and capable. Once again the prince and no longer the man who needed her.

"I would like a shower," he said.

"Me, too, but there's no hot water. At least there wasn't last night."

"The water heater needs to be turned on. I'll take care of that if you want to start on breakfast."

She nodded and followed him out of the room. He didn't even sway as he walked, she thought, amazed by his powers of recovery. As they passed the office, she remembered the telephone and collected it. Reyhan disappeared into a small room behind the pantry while she took the phone out into the courtyard and opened the case so the rising sun would charge the solar cell. Then she took a moment and looked around at the lush, nondesertlike garden in the middle of a three-story sand-and-stone house.

Plants bloomed and trailed everywhere. She couldn't name the various pink, red and white flowers, but she could inhale their sweet fragrance. Water trickled through several fountains and circled the garden before flowing into a stone-lined pond.

No doubt the underground spring was responsible for the flow of water. Emma sighed as she caught sight of a bench in the corner and a small grassy patch. This was a dream house—somewhere she could happily stay forever.

She left the courtyard garden and returned to the kitchen. By the time she'd put together a meal, Reyhan had returned with word that there would soon be hot water. He'd also started the generator.

"We'll have immediate electricity," he said. "We have to use it sparingly until the solar panels start working. Hot water will take an hour or so."

"There's nothing like a day in the desert to make one grateful for the little things," she said, smiling as if being alone with him was no big deal. As if she didn't remember how scared she'd been when she'd found out he'd been shot, and how much he'd hurt her, before they'd left, with his agreement that it was time for her to go home.

As she sat across from him, she tried not to stare at his features. There was no need to memorize his face. Their time together had changed her forever and she would never forget what he looked like. Even now, without a shirt, in need of a shave and less than twenty-four hours after being shot, he still looked masculine, powerful and very princelike.

Silence descended. She searched for a topic to keep the moment from being too awkward.

"Whose house is this?" she asked as she sipped the coffee she'd prepared.

"Mine. It belonged to my aunt. She left it to me when she died."

"This is where you came to after we got married," she said as the pieces of the past clicked into place.

He nodded. "I needed to be here for her funeral

service and then I had to settle her affairs.'' He stared past her, as if seeing into that long-ago time. ''She and I were very close. My parents loved each other more than they loved their children. My brother Jefri didn't seem to mind, but I noticed.'' He shrugged. ''When things were difficult, Sheza was there for me.''

Simple words, she thought, reading the pain behind them. She could imagine a young, lonely prince, growing up in privilege, but without affection. The woman who took his parents' place would always hold a special place in his heart. No wonder he'd been devastated by her loss.

''I'm sorry,'' she said quietly. ''I wish I'd known what you were going through.''

He sipped his coffee. ''It wouldn't have made a difference. I would never have let you comfort me.''

''Why not?''

One corner of his mouth turned up. ''I am Prince Reyhan of Bahania. I am not in need of comforting.''

She leaned toward him. ''I see. And who exactly buys into that line?''

''You would have.''

''You're right. It's something a child would have believed. But I'm not that little girl anymore. Now I know better.''

His dark gaze settled on her face. ''You were very brave yesterday.''

''Not really. At first I was furious at being taken hostage. I knew they'd try to get money from you. They didn't, did they?''

''No. We were able to cancel the transfer. My security chief had a plan to get the money back even if the transfer had gone through. But if necessary, I would have paid.''

"Nice to know," she said, not surprised, but still pleased.

"You are my wife, Emma. I could not let you be harmed."

She didn't feel like his wife. She didn't feel like anything except excess baggage.

"Thank you for saving my life," he said.

"Thank you for saving mine."

"So we are even, which is better than one of us being in debt to another." He smiled. "You did not expect danger to be a part of your visit to Bahania. This experience must make you eager to be back in Dallas."

So much less than he thought. "There are things I'll miss about being here," she told him. Mostly him.

His smile faded. "I'm sorry I hurt you when we were at the palace."

When he'd rejected her, she thought. When he'd turned his back on her offer to make love.

"Yes, well, it's not a big deal."

"I don't believe you," he said. "It was a big deal to both of us. There are things you don't understand."

"Then explain them to me."

He glanced out the window. "There is a legend that the spring that runs under this house is the result of heartache. That a young man got lost in the desert and wandered for days. He was nearly out of water when he found a single blooming plant. So impressed by the beauty of the flower, he poured his last drops of water onto the parched leaves to give it longer life. Grateful, the flower became a beautiful woman. They made love but in the morning, the young man died from dehydration. The woman wept and her tears became a river.''

He turned back to her. ''The garden in the courtyard pays homage to them both. Some of the plants date back nearly a hundred years.''

''That's a very sad story.''

''It is a lesson. We must pay attention to what matters. The young woman possessed magical powers. She could have restored the young man first. Instead she took what she wanted and as a result, lost him.''

She shook her head. ''I think the lesson is to seize whatever love we can find for as long as we have it.''

''Perhaps you are right.'' He rose. ''The hot water should be ready soon. You may shower first.''

As appealing as a shower sounded, she had other things on her mind. Maybe it was stupid to take another chance on him and lay her heart on the line. Maybe she didn't have a choice.

''You don't have to let me go, Reyhan.''

He stiffened slightly and didn't look at her as he spoke. ''Yes, I do.''

''Why? Who is this other woman you plan to marry? What will she give you that I can't?''

''Peace of mind.''

Chapter Fourteen

After her shower, Emma decided to explore the rest of the small palace. Reyhan had settled in the library and after the cryptic end to their breakfast conversation, she wasn't sure what was left to say between them.

She had a thousand questions, but what was new about that? She'd had questions from the beginning—such as why had he married her in the first place and why had he *stayed* married to her? Asking why he had to marry someone else for his peace of mind was way down there on the "questions to ask" priority list.

She climbed to the second story and explored the amazing rooms. There was a large open area that had to be a ballroom, some kind of living room and four incredibly luxurious bedrooms that would rival the elegance of the famous pink palace in the capital city.

Even without any knowledge about antiques, she recognized the beauty of the carved furniture and the glittering gold leaf edging the chairs. There were dressers and armoires and four-poster beds with stairs leading to high mattresses. Amazing murals covered the walls. In one bedroom, she found a pumpkin coach and six horses, all made of crystal. In another there was a carved set of toy soldiers.

On the third floor were more spartan rooms, except for a round room in a tower. Stained-glass windows cast a rainbow of light on the marble floor. The room was completely empty except for a desk with a chest in the middle.

Curious, she crossed to the desk and opened the chest. When she saw what was inside, her breath caught.

There were pictures. Dozens of pictures, all of a young woman. In some she was laughing, in others serious. Sometimes she faced the camera, sometimes she hid her face. One had been taken while she slept.

Emma felt her heart constrict as she recognized a much-younger version of herself. Reyhan had taken these pictures while they'd been dating and then after they'd married.

Below the pictures were mementos from their dates, all the notes she'd written—and several detective reports. She flipped through them and read his messages to the company he'd hired to check on her for the first few months they'd been separated. He'd obviously wanted to know that she was all right. A few pictures of her had been included with the reports and they were as well-worn as the pages of the report.

''I don't understand,'' she whispered into the silence. Why had he done this? Why had he kept everything?

Had he been any other man, she would have thought—hoped—that he cared about her. That she mattered. But he wasn't. He was Prince Reyhan of Bahania and he didn't let himself care.

Or did he? Emma sank onto the floor and studied the detective reports more closely. Reyhan was proud. He would not give his heart easily, nor would he want it toyed with. Had he cared about her and had she not understood the depth of his feelings? He wasn't the kind of man who would marry on a whim. He'd chosen her—only her. Now he didn't want a divorce because he loved someone else but so that he could make a marriage of convenience to produce heirs. He didn't want to fall in love again—was that because he still loved her, or because the first time things had ended so badly?

She thought about all that had happened so long ago. How she'd hidden away from him, like a child afraid of being punished. How she'd let her parents convince her he didn't care because it was easier than confessing her guilty secret.

She claimed to be someone different from that scared young woman, yet was she any more willing to fight for what she wanted? If she loved Reyhan, she needed to tell him. If she wanted a chance at making their marriage work, then she would have to fight for him.

She tossed down the report and scrambled to her feet. She wasn't going to wait another second. They belonged together and she was going to help him see that. No matter how long it took.

She raced down the stairs. Once she reached the main floor, she called out his name as she ran from room to room. She burst into the bedroom he'd been using just as he stepped out of the bathroom.

He wore nothing but a towel, and both it and the bandage were white against his skin. Her throat closed as she remembered the last time they'd been in this position—how he'd rejected her. Determined not to be swayed by fear of rejection and his pride, she squared her shoulders.

"We have to talk," she told him.

His dark eyes burned with a fire she recognized. Her insides quivered slightly and her thighs trembled.

"No."

The single word didn't frighten her. He wasn't going to get his way—not anymore. This was too important to let his pride win. Of course if he really didn't care about her at all, she was about to experience the most humiliating moment of her life, but she had to be willing to risk it all if she wanted to win it all.

"I know you want me," she said, crossing the room to stand directly in front of him.

"Desire means nothing," he told her, turning his back on her. "It is simply a reaction."

"To all women or just to me?" She walked up behind him and placed her hands on his bare shoulders. "What happens when I touch you, Reyhan? I know what happens to me. My insides melt while my whole body starts to ache with a hunger I can barely control.'' She stroked the length of his spine. ''My breathing quickens. There is fire everywhere.''

His skin was smooth, his muscles unyielding. When her fingers reached the edge of the towel, he shuddered.

''You're so sleek and strong,'' she murmured, then pressed a kiss to his back. ''Straight to my curves, hard to my soft. Is it just me?'' she asked. ''Tell me.''

He turned on her with a roar that could have been anger or passion or maybe both. He reached for her and hauled her against him, apparently unaware or unconcerned about his bullet wound.

She was more than willing to ignore it, too, as he kissed her with a need that was even stronger than her own. There were no preliminarily kisses, no soft queries. Instead he took her mouth and claimed her. His lips pressed against hers with a pressure that had her arching against him.

More, she thought frantically as she clung to him and kissed him back. She wanted it all.

His tongue swept over and around hers even as he pushed and tugged at her clothing. She wore only a T-shirt and jeans, but they were too much of a barrier when all she had to do was tug at his towel to undress *him*.

And then he was naked and she didn't worry about her own clothing. Not when she could reach her hand between them and touch his arousal.

As her fingers closed over him, he groaned, then

swore and tore his mouth away. "Get these damn clothes off!" he demanded.

She looked into his eyes and laughed softly. "Impatient, are we?"

"I'll die if I don't have you now."

"Good. Because that's exactly how I feel."

She pulled off her T-shirt and kicked off her sandals while he worked on her jeans. Her bra went next, then she pulled down her panties.

The next second she was falling onto the bed and Reyhan was on top of her.

"I want you," he breathed. "Emma, I need you."

Uncontrollable desire tightened his features. She felt his need, because it was her own. She understood his dilemma even as she reached between them and guided him inside of her.

"You're not ready," he protested, trying to hold back.

She knew she was hot, wet and slick. "Yes, I am."

He plunged into her and they both cried out. Within seconds they were lost in a frenzy of sensation and wanting. She pulled him closer, wanting him deeper. He kissed her eyes, her cheeks, before claiming her mouth. She wrapped her legs around him and as her orgasm approached had to break the kiss to gasp for air.

"Reyhan," she breathed as her body stiffened before convulsing into release.

He continued to fill her over and over until the shudders faded. It was only then that he groaned out her name and was still.

She closed her eyes and let herself relax into his

embrace. Her need for him hadn't faded, only shifted. Now she wanted to be as emotionally connected as they had been physically.

Reyhan withdrew and rolled onto his back, pulling her with him so that she draped across his chest.

"We should not have done that," he said as he stroked her hair.

"Because you're worried about me getting pregnant," she said.

"That is one consideration. Eventually the odds will catch up with us."

They already had. Emma felt time shift and bend and suddenly she was eighteen, alone in her room and crying. Pain filled her body, but not from a physical source. Instead she felt the ache of being alone and so lost, she would never find her way back.

"What?" he asked, continuing to touch her hair. "Where have you gone? I see such sadness in your eyes."

She hadn't been sure she was going to tell him. What was the point? But now, suddenly she wanted him to know. Not to make him feel badly but so that he would understand more.

"I was pregnant before," she whispered. "From our honeymoon."

She braced herself for his violent reaction. She didn't expect him to get angry, but she knew there would be energy and demands for information. Perhaps even accusations. But instead he stayed on the bed, his fingers brushing against her scalp, his other hand tucked behind his head.

"What happened?"

A simple question, yet it was as if he'd unlocked a hidden door. She felt her heart shudder as the memories escaped and raced to the light of day for the first time in six years.

"The doctor said it wasn't uncommon to lose a baby in the first few weeks of pregnancy, especially for a young woman. He said there was probably something wrong with it and that was nature's way of making things right." She blinked to hold back tears, but still they spilled over onto her cheeks. "I was so upset when you left that I locked myself in my room at my parents' house and cried for nearly two weeks. I've always wondered if our child couldn't stand the thought of a mother who was so sad all the time."

"So you take responsibility for what happened?"

She nodded.

"I see." He cupped her cheek. "Perhaps our child didn't want a father who disappeared without word."

"You had nothing to do with me losing the baby."

"Neither did you." His dark gaze locked on her face. "So that is why you refused to see me. You were too upset."

She nodded. "That's a part of it. I was ashamed, too. And scared. I thought you'd be so angry with me."

He wrapped his arms around her and drew her closer until she rested on top of him and they could kiss. He brushed his mouth against hers. "Never. With the wisdom of hindsight I know that I shouldn't have left you behind when my aunt died. I should have brought you with me."

"I'm not sure that would have helped. I couldn't have handled the situation, or you. Not then."

One corner of his mouth turned up. "You think you can handle me now?"

"Yes."

"What makes you so sure?"

This was, as her father would say, where the rubber met the road. How willing was she to risk everything and lay it on the line?

"Because before I didn't know why you'd married me. I was young and scared and too inexperienced to know how to please a man. Everything is different now."

The humor disappeared as if it had never been. He started to sit up. Emma pushed on his shoulders, trying desperately to hold him in place.

"Reyhan, don't. We have to talk about it."

"There is nothing to say."

"I think we could talk for a lifetime and never say all the things we missed by being apart. Reyhan, why didn't you ever tell me you loved me?"

He grasped her by the waist and slid her aside, then sat up. That simple action warned her he was already slipping away.

"Why is it such a horrible thing to admit?" she asked desperately. "Is it because I was so immature? I know I couldn't be a partner for you then, but things are different now. We're *both* different. You loved me then. Couldn't you care a little for me now?"

He didn't speak, didn't move. She wasn't sure he was even breathing.

Frightened, and not sure how to convince him,

mostly because she didn't understand what she was fighting against, she tried to speak from the heart.

"I don't know what I felt back then. I was a kid. I keep saying that but it's true. I had a fantasy about love and marriage and what my husband would be like. You rescued me that very first day and I'm not sure I saw you as a real person. You were more like a superhero or something. But now I can see the man and he's a good and honorable person."

She leaned against Reyhan's back and wrapped her arms around his shoulders.

"You're proud and sometimes that's annoying, but I can live with it," she continued. "I want to stay here with you. I want us to stay married, to love each other and have babies together." She swallowed before confessing her most intimate secret. "I'm in love with you."

Reyhan felt each word. They cut him like knives. When he'd been shot the day before, he'd barely felt the pain, but now, with Emma, he was ripped apart.

Love. She spoke the words he would have sold his soul to hear. Words that would drive him to his knees with gratitude. But then what? Who would he be if he gave in to his love and desire for this woman? How could he be strong? How could he be a man if he was controlled by a woman?

"No!" he roared, and sprang to his feet. "Do not love me. I will not love you in return. Not again. I will not be crushed by the needing and wanting. I will not have you fill my head and consume the very breath from my body. I will not be made weak by all that I feel for you."

He glared at her, but she didn't flinch. Instead she met his angry gaze with a look so filled with love that he could have captured the emotion in his hand and trapped it in a box.

"It doesn't have to be like that," she said as she stood naked in front of him. Her long hair spread across her shoulders and teased the top of her breasts. "We can support each other, gaining strength from what the other gives. A team is better than a single man. I want to make you happy, Reyhan. I want to be the one person in the world you can trust with everything and I want to trust you the same way."

He knew what she asked, what she wanted. He knew the truth—it was better to be safe and alone. Better to walk away.

He started to do just that, but before he did so, he allowed himself one last look at her. He took in her beautiful face, the slight tilt of her eyes and the fullness of her mouth. He memorized the sound of her laugh and how she scowled when she was angry. He pictured her hair up, as she'd worn it to the formal reception at the palace.

His gaze dropped lower to her full breasts, the tight nipples that called to him like a siren. Wanting stirred, but he ignored it. Next he studied her narrow waist and the fullness of her hips. He felt badly about the child they'd lost, about the pain she'd suffered alone. Had she been recovering when he'd first tried to see her? Her father had said she was ill. Reyhan had assumed the old man was lying, but perhaps not.

They hadn't used birth control. Why hadn't he considered the possibility of her having his child?

A son, he thought with regret. Or a pretty little girl of five who ran through the halls of the palace and wrapped him around her finger as much as he would wrap her around his heart.

Standing there naked, with sunlight filling the room, Reyhan felt the weight of all he'd lost when he'd abandoned Emma, and the weight of it made it impossible for him to stand. He sank to his knees.

She was at his side in an instant.

"Don't let me go," she pleaded. "We've been given a second chance. Can't you see how rare and precious that is?"

He clung to her because she was as she had always been—his lifeline. He had tried to live without her. He had convinced himself a cold gray world was a safe place to be, but it was not living. It was an existence that offended those brave enough to reach for what they wanted.

"I am a man humbled by a woman," he said, taking her face in his hands and kissing her.

"I am the one who is humbled," she breathed as she kissed him over and over again. "I love you, Reyhan. For always."

"And I love you. From the first moment I saw you."

He drew her into his arms then carried her to the bed where he settled both of them on the tangled sheets.

"Stay with me," he pleaded. "Love me. Have my children, work at my side, fill my nights and my heart."

Tears spilled out of the corners of her eyes. "Yes. For always."

He wrapped his arms around her. Emma could feel the steady beating of his heart. His skin was warm against her own, both comforting and arousing.

There was much to discuss, she thought as she snuggled closer still. Where they would make their home—either here or the pink palace. How often she would be visiting her parents in Texas. What Reyhan was going to say when she told him she loved her work too much to give it up. While being a delivery room nurse would be difficult, she would have to find another way to use her skills.

Last, and perhaps most important, she wondered when she would tell him about the tiny life growing inside of her. She knew with the certainty that had served women well since the dawn of time that they had made a baby that morning. A child who would be the first of many. The new life was their promise to each other—that they would love with all their hearts. Having nearly lost everything, they would hold on to each other while nurturing a love as constant and endless as the desert itself.

* * * * *

If you enjoyed what you just read,
then we've got an offer you can't resist!

Take 2 bestselling love stories FREE!

Plus get a FREE surprise gift!

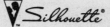